Love You,
Hate You

Love You, Hate You

BALLET SCHOOL CONFIDENTIAL

CHARIS MARSH

DUNDURN
TORONTO

Editor: Nicole Chaplin
Design: Jennifer Scott
Printer: Webcom

Library and Archives Canada Cataloguing in Publication

Marsh, Charis
  Love you, hate you / by Charis Marsh.

Also issued in electronic format.
ISBN 978-1-55488-961-7

  I. Title.

PS8626.A7665L69 2011   jC813'.6   C2011-901858-6

1   2   3   4   5   15   14   13   12   11

Conseil des Arts du Canada   Canada Council for the Arts   Canadä   ONTARIO ARTS COUNCIL   CONSEIL DES ARTS DE L'ONTARIO

We acknowledge the support of the Canada Council for the Arts and the Ontario Arts Council for our publishing program. We also acknowledge the financial support of the Government of Canada through the Canada Book Fund and Livres Canada Books, and the Government of Ontario through the Ontario Book Publishing Tax Credit and the Ontario Media Development Corporation.

Care has been taken to trace the ownership of copyright material used in this book. The author and the publisher welcome any information enabling them to rectify any references or credits in subsequent editions.

J. Kirk Howard, President

Printed and bound in Canada.
www.dundurn.com

Dundurn
3 Church Street, Suite 500
Toronto, Ontario, Canada
M5E 1M2

Gazelle Book Services Limited
White Cross Mills
High Town, Lancaster, England
LA1 4XS

Dundurn
2250 Military Road
Tonawanda, NY
U.S.A. 14150

For my family, who have always supported my dance addiction:

Mum, Dad, Riel, Willow, Gage, Seger, River, Grandpa, and Grandpam.

Chapter One

Kaitlyn Wardle
OMG, so excited, going to the Vancouver International Ballet Academy, top level, on full scholarship!!!

Kaitlyn sighed impatiently, fiddling with the straps on her bag. Today was her first day at the globally renowned Vancouver International Ballet Academy, and her mom was taking forever to park. Cecilia Wardle had insisted on coming in to talk to Mr. and Mrs. Demidovski about "what they could expect in the following year," but Kaitlyn was dreading walking into the academy with her mother.

"Mom, I'm on full scholarship," Kaitlyn tried to argue, yet again. "I don't think they're going to not cast me. And I'm fourteen! You don't need to come in."

"Kaitlyn, last year you were Sugarplum Fairy," Cecilia's tone was firm. "Mr. and Mrs. Demidovski promised they would make sure that you were challenged if you came to the academy, and I am going to make sure that that happens."

"Okay, okay," Kaitlyn groaned. "I'm just kind of nervous about going to the academy. Everybody is super skinny here."

"Well, you can be, too, Kaitlyn, if you just worked at it. And don't forget that nobody here has technique like you, or a resume like yours." Kaitlyn smiled to herself. She might want to lose ten — no twenty — pounds, but her technique was untouchable. Why, yesterday she had done nine pirouettes on *pointe*! Anybody who thought they could beat her was depending on "artistry." She pulled down the visor mirror and adjusted a few pins in her bun. It was a perfect flat circle, and her lucky pink ribbon lay flat against the bun, the bow perfectly centred.

"Kaitlyn, come on," Cecilia said impatiently as she waited outside the car.

As they walked into the academy, Kaitlyn let herself fall behind her mother. The entrance led directly into a hallway. Kaitlyn and Cecilia paused there, looking around for someone to ask where to go. The whole of one side of the hallway was covered in mirrors. It was more than most people could do not to walk down the hallway staring at their reflections. The mirrors changed every few feet, distorting your reflection with each step, so you were never really sure what you actually looked like.

Gabriel, the office manager, suddenly appeared beside them, giving Kaitlyn a little start. He gestured at her mother, "Come, come, Mr. and Mrs. Demidovski are waiting!"

Kaitlyn liked him. He was a rather large, good-natured man with a tendency to disappear if you were looking for him. He'd sometimes pretend that he didn't speak English if he didn't like what you were saying. It rather hard to believe, though, since he was from Vancouver, but he did not seem to think it fair that the rest of the staff at the academy had that option and he did not.

Gabriel ushered Cecilia into the office and shooed Kaitlyn on her way before he closed the door. Kaitlyn shrugged, squared her shoulders, took a deep breath, and continued down the stairs and to the changing rooms. She had been to summers at the academy before, so she knew the way. The fluorescent lighting in the changing rooms hadn't gotten any less abrasive since the last time she'd been here. Kaitlyn walked into the bathroom. *It's definitely gotten worse in here,* she thought. She smiled at the girls doing their hair by the mirror. "So, which bathroom works?"

"Oh my God, it's Kaitlyn!" Taylor screamed and ran over to hug Kaitlyn enthusiastically.

Kaitlyn laughed, her eyebrows raised. "Taylor, tone down the excitement, hon."

Taylor hugged her again. "But, Kaitlyn, I'm sooooo happy that you've *finally* come to the academy! We are totally going to have so much fun together! This year is going to be awesome!"

"Uh huh ..." drawled Kaitlyn, wanting to give Taylor a set down. At that moment, though, she glanced up and saw Anna staring down at her, her eyebrows raised and a smirk on her face. At five foot eight, Anna was six inches taller than Kaitlyn and a lot skinnier. Kaitlyn turned to Taylor. "Right, this year is going to be so much fun!" she said mockingly and went to change, fuming. *Anna is so annoying,* Kaitlyn thought. *She is good at ballet, but not nearly as good as me, and she's older! Just because she's gorgeous and seriously rich, she thinks she can do whatever she likes.*

Kaitlyn came out and looked in the mirror. *Front, check. Profile, yuck.* The academy's uniforms had been specially ordered, and they'd obviously gotten a good deal: the uniforms continued straight from the back to the butt, creating a pocket of air where there should have been a waist. Kaitlyn sighed just as Taylor came out of the stall.

"You need a hip alignment belt, Kaitlyn, everyone has one. I'd loan you mine, but I'm, like, so tiny! Sorry!" she giggled.

"Okay, Taylor," Kaitlyn said, rolling her eyes. She went upstairs, finding it difficult to navigate through the bodies sprawled all over them. Some of the Japanese students were huddled at the top of the stairs. Kaitlyn stopped to see what they were doing.

"Ahh, ah, *eti*!" yelled the Japanese boy in the centre of the group.

One of the Japanese girls told him to "Be quiet, Kageki!" For some reason, this caused them all to start giggling, talking even faster than before. Kaitlyn laughed: they were trying to pluck his eyebrows. She continued to the entrance, where the schedule was. *Oh my God! Why are they still here? They are like twenty-one!* She thought, looking at the two girls in front of the board.

Sophia was ranting about the schedule, pacing back in forth in front of it, arms flailing dramatically. "They can't just say, 'rehearsal nine to nine on Sunday!' It's three *months* before the show. What if we have *lives?* What if we have *plans?* Do they think they own us? What is *wrong* with them?!"

Ella yawned, looking down at her nails with exaggerated interest. They were three shades of pink with blue tips, and silver designs all over them, with rhinestones to complete the effect. "It's the academy," she said, yawning again. She looked in the mirror to see what she looked like yawning, then tried it again, this time attempting to do it with pouted lips. "When have they ever been *organized?* They don't believe in lives."

"Excuse me," Kaitlyn said, trying to see the schedule between the two of them.

"Oh, it's you," Sophia said. "When did *you* come?"

"Why are you staring at me?" Ella asked in her intensely practised otherworldly voice. She held up her hand and looked at Kaitlyn through her fingers.

"I just want to … see … the schedule," said Kaitlyn, holding her ground.

"God, don't make such a fuss over it!" Sophia said, moving slightly away. Sophia turned to Ella. "Do you *believe* some people? Like, what's her problem? Some people are just so *rude!*"

"I know," Ella said with a world-weary sigh, as she floated down the hall after Sophia.

Kaitlyn went into Studio A, chose a spot at the front, and self-consciously sat down to warm up. Kaitlyn was naturally flexible (well, she was double jointed pretty much everywhere), so she felt that she didn't really have to stretch. She built muscles easily, and kept them. But this created bulky muscles. Instead of stretching, Kaitlyn flopped into the middle splits and covertly looked around the room, watching everyone else as they stretched and talked.

Jessica was standing off to the side, across from Kaitlyn, staring at the mirror. Turning to profile, she took off her warm-up shirt and tried to stick her spine out as far as she could. Straightening up and frowning slightly, she pulled her warm-up pants below her butt, and then looked at profile again. Turning around and peering over her shoulder, she stared at her butt from the back. Next, Jessica took her pants all the way off, and stood first in the skinny mirror, then in the fat mirror, and then one leg in both to compare. She went and stood next to Taylor, who was the skinniest person in the class. Taylor was facing front, so she looked front too, comparing their reflections. She was wider, so she went to the back of the class and put her warm-ups away, sulking. A couple seconds later, Jessica marched back to the front and took a spot at the front of the *barre*, in front of Mao. She stood there, experimenting with sucking her pelvis and stomach in and out.

Kaitlyn flopped onto her stomach still in the splits, giving her an excuse to hide her laughter. She'd met Jessica at a master class before, but hadn't gotten a chance to appreciate just how messed she was.

Delilah was sitting on the floor stretching with Tristan, both of them giggling quietly about someone. Mr. Moretti walked in, disturbing Kaitlyn's observation as he called, "Everyone, the *barre*, now. Boys, bring the centre *barres* out." He frowned, looking around him. "Where is George?"

"Having a smoke!" Delilah called out.

"Coming, coming, no need to make a big fuss," George said, as he sat down at the piano, shuffling his notes, and taking a quick gulp of his coffee.

"Yes, I suppose it does not matter if the class starts on time … or indeed if we start at all, does it, George?" asked Mr. Moretti, raising his eyebrows.

"Well now, I wouldn't say that. Why don't we just get started now?" George refused to rise to the bait.

"Yes, why don't we do that," replied Mr. Moretti smoothly. "Everyone, are you *cold*? Surely not. Take off your pants and sweaters, how do you expect me to see what your hipses are doing with all those clothes on?"

"I cringe every time he says 'hipses,'" Sophia whispered to Ella.

"Everyone, same *pliés* as always. Oh, congratulations, De-Li-Lah! How far along?" Mr. Moretti bent down to pat her stomach. Delilah blushed and pulled her stomach in more.

The door opened and Anna slipped in. "Sorry, Mr. Moretti, I was just talking to Mr. Demidovski."

"Of *course*, Anna, of course. Take your spot." said Mr. Moretti, frowning.

"Somebody looks pissed," giggled Anna as she slipped in between Tristan and Delilah, commanding her, "Delilah, move up." Delilah did, forcing Mao to work on an angle, and Jessica to work at 45 degree extensions every time she went to the back. The door opened again, and Mrs. Demidovski came in.

"Everyone! Excuse me, Mr. um ... yes. Everyone! Meeting after first class, no *pointe* class today," she said. "Continue," she added before walking out of the room.

"Thank you, Mrs. Demidovski," Mr. Moretti pasted a smile on his face and bowed slightly. "Everyone, next class I expect *pointe* shoes from the beginning. For me, this must be so. For the other teachers, I do not care what they do. *Tendues,* please. Mao, can you demonstrate the exercise for the class?"

Mao began doing the exercise while counting aloud, "One, two, three, four, five, shix ..."

"Shix? What is shix?" asked Mr. Moretti, while the class giggled. Mao looked up at him fearfully and pointed her foot more. When that didn't work she turned out her leg more, and began doing *tendues* with exaggerated roll through. "All right, six," relented Mr. Moretti.

At three o'clock, George began fidgeting. He stacked his notes twice, pretending to organize them. Finally, he stood up and turned around to look at the clock behind him. He gave an exaggerated start of surprise, and turned back to Mr. Moretti. "Hey man, you know this class ends at three?"

Mr. Moretti turned to stare at him. "If you want to leave, George, I'm not stopping you. Feel free to go if you want."

George raised his eyebrows, returning his stare. "Uh, no, that's okay ... I'm just saying ... it's three."

"I believe I say when this class is finished, George. That's my job. But if you want to leave, I'm not stopping you. We can use a CD player. At a least a CD player does not talk."

Angela obviously thought this was hilarious. As Mr. Moretti passed by her, she reached out and put her hand on his shoulder, and said, "Good one!" in a stage whisper.

Mr. Moretti froze. Kaitlyn held her breath as Mr. Moretti turned around and glared at Angela. "I am *not* your friend," he enunciated slowly. He turned away from her and gave a shudder of revulsion. With obvious effort, he recovered himself and began to lead another exercise to the class. George made himself small behind the piano, doing his best impression of a CD player.

After class, Kaitlyn turned to Taylor. "What's the meeting about?"

Jonathon must have overheard, because he laughed. He was from Montana and it was his third year. "Oh, it'll pretty good ... um, a bit of 'this year is going to be different,' a bit of 'we do everything for the student' from Mr. Demidovski, some random shit, and then we clap."

"Sounds fun...." said Kaitlyn, sarcastically. She looked at him more interestedly as he turned away. Jonathon definitely wasn't a stellar dancer, but he looked pretty strong.... Yes, she'd try to get a *pas* with him for competition this year. She stepped up beside him so he looked at her. "So, how do you like it in Canada?" she asked, suddenly friendly. "You look like you could have gotten into some of the big schools like SFB, what made you come here?"

"Oh, I like Canada, so I decided to come to Vancouver," he said easily, not noticing any flattery. "You're pretty good yourself," he added as an afterthought.

"Thanks," said Kaitlyn smiling. "Dumbass," she thought to herself. Did he actually think he was as good as her? They all went into Studio A and waited.

Angela turned to Kaitlyn. "Where are you from?" she asked brightly.

"Oh, here. Van-city." said Kaitlyn, bored.

"Oh. I'm from England and Australia, but I was born here." said Angela. Kaitlyn showed no signs of asking her to elaborate, but she continued anyway. "My Papa," at this Kaitlyn raised her eyebrows in disbelief. Papa? Happy at having engaged Kaitlyn's interest, she thought, Angela gained more enthusiasm for her subject. "My Papa is a diplomat, so we all move around quite a lot. But I just love ballet so much, it is my life."

I think I'm going to puke, Kaitlyn thought.

"So my Mama and Papa promised I could come here by myself."

"Oh. You mean you homestay? Most people here do. Which homestay do you stay at?" said Kaitlyn.

"Oh, I don't homestay! I stay with some family members, but they are not very welcoming ..." she said, trying to look pitiful.

"Oh." said Kaitlyn, not terribly impressed. At that moment the Demidovskis finally came in and Angela shut up, trying to sit up extremely straight and putting a "good student" expression on her face. Kaitlyn looked at her in disbelief.

"Wow, pathetic much," she whispered to Tristan, who had scooted to sit beside her.

"No kidding," he said. "As if the Demidovskis would even look at her. Did you see her in class today?"

"No, how was she?" giggled Kaitlyn. "I mean the Mr. Moretti thing was pretty impressive, but I never actually saw her dance."

"She dances like an obese, deaf person doing hip hop," whispered Tristan. They quickly pulled apart as Mr. Demidovski entered the studio. Mr. Demidovski walked slowly to the front of the room and stood there until the room was completely silent. "My students," he began. Mrs. Demidovski started to cough, and Mr. Demidovski turned to glare at her. "Mrs. Demidovski, I am speaking," he said firmly.

"Sorry," said Mrs. Demidovski, not looking terribly sorry, as she sat down. "Kageki, bring me water please."

"My students," continued Mr. Demidovski. "Welcome. Welcome to my school. Welcome the new students!" Everyone clapped obediently. "We have much of the great dancers from my academy. They are at the Royal Ballet! The top companies in the States! They are in Asia! They dance everywhere! That is because ... they receive the very great training at my school. Always, I give to the students, everything is for the students. Mr. Demidovski gives the sweat, he gives the heart! I give you the inspiration. But for the inspiration, you must give me more! I give you 55 percent the inspiration, the love, the feeling. You must give me ... 110 percent! The students are from all over the world, we have many of the overseas students, from Japan, Australia, China, England, Brazil, Russia. Everyone clap for the overseas students!"

"Mr. Demidovski! You forget the States," Mrs. Demidovski interrupted.

"It is my very great wish, my dream, that you all become great dancers. But this is up to you. The teacher cannot do it for you. The teachers at my academy, they sweat, they give you the love, the inspiration, the work, but they cannot do it all for you. You, you must work hard, you must take care of the physical, make straight, strong, the long, thin line. My students, you must respect all of the teachers, be nice to all of them. I want my students to be more down-to-the-earth. Mr. Demidovski knows that you want to do this. Thank you my students, you give me the love, I love you all. Everyone at my academy, we give the love to each other." Everyone clapped.

"Okay, finish. Everyone, go home!" said Mr. Demidovski.

The younger class went running out of the classroom, glad to be free, except two of them.

"Hello," said a small boy, about eleven. He was smiling at Kaitlyn.

"Uh, hey," she answered, raising her eyebrows in surprise. She recognized him from competition, but there was no way she was going to let him know that.

"My name's Michael. I've been going to the academy for a while now," he spoke with the air of someone offering very confidential information. "This is my friend, Chloe. We're also partners for competition. We're going to win, because everyone else sucks in the junior *pas* category this year. But I just wanted to say we both think that you're amazing, and my mother wanted me to tell you that she's very happy that you decided to go to the academy. She thinks you will bring up the standard of the school. And I just wanted to say, if you notice anything in my dancing that you could correct, please tell me." Michael widened his eyes as far as possible.

"Oh, for sure!" said Kaitlyn. "I'm sure that you and Chloe will do great at comp this year. My mom said you did well last year."

"Thanks!" said Michael. Chloe smiled at her and then followed Michael out. Kaitlyn smiled to herself. The little ones knew to suck up to her, that was a good sign. Her mom would be pleased to hear about that. As she went downstairs, Kaitlyn smelled the lost and found box. *What on earth is in there?* The smell was disgusting. She started digging to find out.

"Hey, watcha doing?" asked Delilah.

"Trying to find out what's stinking up the whole basement!" Kaitlyn replied. Delilah bent down to help.

"Whooee, it *does* stink in here. Oh, look, a brand new pair of *pointe* shoes! Keiko, aren't these yours? They're sewn folded over instead of burned…. Oh, and these are your warm-ups, Jessica …" As Delilah passed out the discoveries, Kaitlyn reached in and pulled out a bag.

"Omigod!" she screamed. "It's a bag of rotting Duan's takeout! Eww! There's another bag of it and an apple!"

"I think there might actually be a janitor!" Delilah said in mock surprise. "We thought there wasn't, but somebody must have put those bags in the lost and found."

Kaitlyn grimaced in disgust and hurried to the bathroom to wash her hands. Anna was going through Taylor's stash of junk food, trying to find something partially healthy, while Taylor stood nervously by watching her.

"How come you have that much junk in your locker?" Kaitlyn asked.

"Well, I, like, always forget to have breakfast and pack a lunch, and I always need to eat before dance, and my mom gets *so* mad when I eat junk, so I store it in my locker and I eat it here where she can't find it. Honestly, she is such a control freak, but I won't tell her where my locker is. I always tell her I need to get home right away to do homework when she asks where it is." Taylor stood up and walked straight into the wall. "*OMG*, I just, like, raped the wall! My boobs totally violated that wall!" Taylor said, giggling as she went into the bathroom.

"Wow, somebody's had too many energy drinks," Kaitlyn said as she left the changing room to go home, muscles aching.

"Hey, you bussing?" asked a boy from her class who'd been sitting out because of his ankle.

"No, my mom's coming to pick me up, but I have to wait for a little bit," replied Kaitlyn. "I'm Kaitlyn, by the way."

"Julian," he answered. "I'm new here."

"Me too," smiled Kaitlyn. "Are you from Van-city?"

"Um, no, I'm sort of from the Island." he answered. "But I've been living in Toronto for the last year with my stepdad. I just moved back to B.C. to go to the academy. I'm homestaying with Mr. Yu. It's totally cool, but the

Love You, Hate You

food sucks majorly. I'm going to McKinley Secondary for my half-day academics. Where do you go?"

"Oh, I go to McKinley too, but my mom picked me up and drove me here because it was the first day. I'm going to bus tomorrow, though."

"That's cool. See you tomorrow then. *Konbanwa!*" he said, grinning.

"What does *that* mean?"

"'Good evening.' Keiko, my homestay sister, taught me some Japanese last night. I'm the only person there who likes speaking English, and Leon speaks Spanish, Keiko and Mao like Japanese, and the Yus like Mandarin, so it's kind of lonely at the dinner table," he said, pouting.

Kaitlyn laughed. "I can totally picture that. I'm glad my parents live here."

"Oh no!" Julian said in exaggerated horror. "Homestaying totally rocks. I mean, you get to live with a bunch of other teenagers, leave school way early to dance, and the Yus don't care what you do with your free time as long as you tell them when you don't need dinner."

Cecilia was coming down the hall quickly, gesturing at Kaitlyn to get up. "Come on, Kaitlyn, let's go."

"Kay, bye then," laughed Kaitlyn.

"Bye," Julian smiled. He swung his long body out of the chair and sauntered down the hall, plugging in his iPod earbuds as he went.

As Kaitlyn and Cecilia walked to the car, Kaitlyn felt a little burst of happiness spread through her body. Her first day at the academy was over, and it hadn't been so bad. Julian seemed sweet, and Taylor would be

21

easy to boss around. Anna was the only one who had got more corrections from Mr. Moretti, and her corrections were mostly of the "how many times do I have to tell you?" variety, so Kaitlyn felt confident that she would pass her soon.

As soon as they got in the car, Cecilia asked, "Well? How was it?"

"Fine. Mr. Moretti likes me, I think, and Taylor's trying to be friends with me, so I have someone to talk to."

"Yes, well, Kaitlyn, you can't rely on just Taylor. You're going to have to make some friends who are actually good dancers. What about Anna? Does she still not like you?"

Kaitlyn sighed. "Yeah, and she's totally one of the Demidovskis' favourites. She was even late for class today because she was talking to Mr. Demidovski. But I'm better than her. It's just her body type. Oh, and Michael and Chloe came up to me today. Michael said that his mom said that I was going to bring up the standard of the academy, and asked me to give him corrections."

"Well that's great, Kaitlyn! If Michael's mom said that, it means everyone already knows that the Demidovskis like you. I'm very pleased by that. And don't worry, sweetie. You're the best they have right now. Anna is nothing, neither is Taylor. Did you happen to hear if Alexandra has made the finals at Genee? "

"No, Mom, I was a little *busy!*" Kaitlyn snapped.

"Okay, sweetie, calm down. You just need some sleep. What do you want for dinner? A salad? Do you want to stop by Whole Foods?"

"I'd rather eat some pasta," Kaitlyn muttered under her breath, then added aloud, "Sure mom, whatever. Just hurry up, please. I need to cover my books and write 500 words on 'what I want to accomplish in socials this year,' tonight."

Kaitlyn went to her room and flopped on the bed. *To Tylenol or not to Tylenol, that is the question,* she thought grumpily. Coming back to dance after the break between summer intensives and school-year classes was always annoying, but Kaitlyn just hadn't been able to force herself to take drop-in classes at Harbour during the two week break. She reached over and logged on to her laptop. As she signed on to MSN she grimaced. *I'm going to have to change my email before anyone at the academy adds me!* Ballerina_babee@live.ca *isn't very original.*

She started her homework—"Oh, forget it," she said out loud. *How am I supposed to concentrate on my homework when all I can think about is the academy?* She logged on to Facebook. Ten friend requests. Kaitlyn giggled. Obviously she *had* danced well today.

Taylor's chat box popped up, "Hey!"

Kaitlyn groaned. She didn't want to talk to Taylor right now, but it would probably be diplomatic if she pretended they were BFFs for now.

* * *

The alarm started blasting, and Kaitlyn quickly turned it off. She had been awake for a couple of minutes anyway. She always did that the first week of school. As she got dressed, she felt happy and excited. She lost a pound yesterday, and she hadn't even been that hungry. She loved adrenalin: it usually had that affect on her. *Maybe I can lose two pounds today!* She looked at herself in the mirror. *I look pretty good. I might not be able to dress as expensively as Anna, but I do look younger. And really,* she thought, *isn't that more important for dance, anyway?*

When she got downstairs, Cecilia already had her breakfast ready: a bowl of porridge and fat-free yogurt sitting on the table with her bagged lunch.

"Your dad's going to drive you today, Kaitlyn," Cecilia said. "Were you talking to Taylor last night?"

"Yes, why?"

"Oh, I was on your Facebook, and her status said she was looking forward to her birthday party...."

"Yeah, she invited me to it last night. It's going to be at a restaurant downtown on the twentieth," said Kaitlyn, putting some sugar and milk on her porridge.

"We'll get you a new dress for it then. Have a good day. Remember to get to the front of the class and keep Mr. Moretti correcting you, he's doing most of the casting for *The Nutcracker* this year. Mr. Demidovski told me that he's thinking of you as Clara, but if you impress Mr. Moretti you might get Sugarplum."

"Okay, okay, Mom! Geez!" Kaitlyn went to find her dad, who was on the computer, finishing up an email. "Dad, we have to *go*, like, now."

"All right Kaitlyn, go wait in the car. I'll be there in a sec," Jeff Wardle said, still typing. Sighing, Kaitlyn went to wait.

As they drove to McKinley, Jeff asked how her first day at the academy had been.

"It was good."

"Did you like the teachers?" Jeff asked as he turned onto Granville and nearly ran over a homeless man who was racing across the street.

"Dad!" laughed Kaitlyn. "No one *likes* ballet teachers, they're all crazy."

"Okay, but did you learn anything?"

"Um, the one I had yesterday was okay," said Kaitlyn, as they pulled into the school parking lot. "He's Italian, so he doesn't teach Balanchine. I like that."

"Okay, have a good day. Good luck!" Jeff said as Kaitlyn left the car.

"Thanks, I'll need it!"

After school everyone met up at the bus stop to go to the academy.

"Hey, 'sup? How was school?" asked Julian, smiling at Kaitlyn. He seemed rather relieved to see her.

Delilah turned to Kaitlyn; "Don't you think he would make a good drag queen?" she pointed at Julian. "I mean, he has such awesome hair!"

"I can see," Kageki said, grinning.

"How do you even know what a drag queen is?" said Anna. "Who taught you that word?"

"Tristan," Kageki was laughing. "He taught me so many good words I want to use, but he says I can't use. Like …"

"Shh!" Julian laughed as he covered Kageki's mouth. Kaitlyn just stood there laughing at Kageki. He looked so funny with his ultra-fashionable haircut. There were different chunks of hair going every which way: some parts perfectly straight, others in corkscrew curls. The affect was accentuated by the fact that his hair was dyed red.

"What are *you* laughing at?" asked Anna, suddenly turning to Kaitlyn.

"Nothing!" said Kaitlyn, too surprised to think of a good come back. Just at that moment, the bus drove up and they got on.

"Aren't you kids leaving school a little early?" the bus driver asked, raising his eyebrows.

"No, we're in the Super Achievers Program," said Delilah, smiling sweetly up at him.

"What's *that*?" he asked.

"It's for sports and arts. We get to leave at 11:30 every day to go to dance, and we get fine arts and P.E credits for it," said Anna, looking at him as if he was an idiot.

"Oh, all right," he said, looking sorry he'd asked. "School's sure different from when I was there," he muttered to himself.

"God, isn't Taylor the most retarded person on the planet?' Anna said as they sat down, staring straight at Kaitlyn.

Kaitlyn tried to ignore her. *FML,* she thought.

Everyone had sat down on the back benches, but there were no more seats there, so Kaitlyn either had to stand the whole ride and look like a desperate idiot, or sit in one of the forward-facing benches and turn around the whole ride. She picked sitting in the forward-facing benches.

"Oh, Jonathon told me that Alexandra has made finals, and is … is going? Sorry, coming, back in two days," said Kageki.

"That's awesome she made it to finals!" Kaitlyn said. "The Demidovskis must be really happy."

"Oh, I doubt they know," laughed Delilah.

"Wouldn't Alexandra have phoned them?" Kaitlyn asked.

"God, why?" said Delilah. "She doesn't owe them anything."

"I think she should have phoned them," said Angela, who was sitting quietly in the corner. "After all, they let her go to the Genee."

"Let her?" snorted Anna. "You mean they 'let' her go try to win something for them, so they could have more students come to the 'globally renowned Vancouver International Ballet Academy,' while they didn't lift a finger to help her prepare?"

"They did give her some privates…" Angela blushed and sank lower into her seat.

"Yeah, for like a hundred bucks an hour after she begged. *And* they showed up late for them," Delilah chimed in, probably hoping to get on Anna's good side. Anna just looked annoyed. She didn't need help to squash Angela.

Kaitlyn turned on her iPod and faced front, glad that she didn't get a seat in the back. Now she had an excuse to zone out. She daydreamed, half-listening to the conversation behind her, mostly to make sure it wasn't about her, through the sounds of the Thriving Ivory. She could see herself winning gold at Prix de Lausanne and going to the Royal Ballet. Anna would be so jealous and would have to suck up to her, couldn't get a job *anywhere*. And she was dating a boy in the company who was perfect, and so strong and nice. In her daydream, she was so happy that she just didn't need to eat, so she had a perfect body type, she even grew a couple of inches.... Kaitlyn sighed happily and escaped reality for the rest of the ride to the academy.

Chapter Two

Taylor Audley
I'm Sooooo hapy that my bff Kaitlyn has come to the acadimy, and that my b-day party is soon!!!! Exited for Nut auditshions!

Taylor woke up feeling surprisingly rested. She tried to remember why. *I'm sure it's Wednesday, not Sunday. Am I sick and forgot? I don't feel sick …* She stumbled into the kitchen, head rushing.

"Mom, why am I still here?" she asked, falling into a chair.

"You have *Nutcracker* auditions today, Taylor. And you were up so late talking to that nice boy from your school. What's his name…? Brandon," Charlize Petrenko said. "I wanted to make sure you had enough sleep."

"Oh," said Taylor, "I didn't know that they were today."

"I told you Taylor," Charlize sounded annoyed. "Oopsies," she giggled, spilling milk on the table. "I told you last night. You never remember anything. Do you want a meal replacement shake?" She took one for herself.

"No!" said Taylor, averting her eyes. Meal replacement shakes always made her feel sick in the morning.

"Well, do you want some cereal then? There's some Rice Krispies."

"Do we have any Froot Loops, Mom?"

"Yes, but don't put any sugar on them, Taylor, they have enough sugar as it is," Charlize sighed. "Oh, and Taylor, your dad wants you to call him. He wants to know if you're going to stay with him for Christmas."

"How should I know?" asked Taylor, pouring a cup of cereal in a bowl, carefully adding five heaping tablespoons of white sugar and some milk. She eyed the bowl suspiciously. It still didn't look very appetizing. She added some spray whipping cream and some red sprinkles which happened to be in her bathrobe.

"Taylor.... Oh, why do I even try?" Charlize groaned, throwing her hands in the air. Taylor ignored her and started eating the sprinkles off the whipping cream.

"Ta-aylor! I can't believe you *just* ate the whipping cream off the cereal!"

"The cereal was *soggy*! I can't eat it when it's mushy!"

"Whatever, we have to go *now*. You have your audition."

As Charlize drove Taylor to the academy, she kept up a steady stream of advice: "Remember to smile at all the teachers today, and do your hair nicely. Most of what people think when they see people dance is what they look like. Put some lipstick or gloss on, you look washed out. I told you to get to sleep last night!"

"Mom, geez, shut up already! And it's not all about what I look like you know, it's about other stuff, too, like technique!" Taylor said angrily. Charlize continued as if she hadn't heard her.

"Don't eat the junk you usually do. It just makes you more ADD. You should wear your red bodysuit so you stand out. And please remember that Kaitlyn is *not* your friend, she wants a good part just as much as you do, and her mother stops at nothing to make sure she gets it." She pulled out her wallet as they reached a red light. "Here's twenty-five dollars for the audition and a twenty for dinner and lunch. I really mean it, Taylor, you need to concentrate and try to get a good part. Did you know that Kaitlyn is on full scholarship? If you would just improve a little faster, Taylor, I know you could do it. And you have to, Honey, because you sure aren't going to make it to university." Taylor turned the car music on as loud as she could without going deaf, and pretended she couldn't hear her mother telling her to turn it down.

When her mother finally turned the music down, Taylor said, "I don't know what is wrong with you, I *do* work as hard as I can, and Kaitlyn is just a suck-up. I hate her smile. And I'm not going to wear the red bodysuit, it makes my boobs look too big. I left it at home, anyway."

"Oh, Taylor, you forgot your red bodysuit?"

"No, I am just not going to friggin' wear it! I'm going to wear my blue one. I like that one."

"Okay, Taylor. I'm just trying to help!" Charlize said as they pulled up beside the academy.

"Well, stop it!" said Taylor as she got out of the car.

"Wait, I'm coming in! I want to talk to Cecilia."

"Who?" said Taylor.

"Kaitlyn's mother."

"Oh, great," Taylor grimaced.

"Did you remember to invite Kaitlyn to your birthday party?"

"Yes, Mom!" answered Taylor.

"Oh, and Taylor, do you know if Alexandra going to be back for casting today?"

"I. Don't. Know," Taylor stalked off. As she walked into the academy, Keiko came excitedly up to her.

"Tay-chan, guess what?! Alexandra got bronze at Genee!"

"Wow, that's sweet!" said Taylor excitedly. "Is she back yet?"

"*Hai,*" said Keiko. "She's downstairs changing. She's super skinny right now. Like, bone, bone, bone."

"Oh, good for her," said Taylor.

Keiko grimaced. "No, not like good, good skinny, you know? Like, not so good, I don't think it is nice. But is useful to get bronze! Come downstairs with me to get changed."

"Okay," said Taylor smiling. "Are we auditioning with the youth company, or is it just level A and B?" Taylor whispered as they walked down the hallway.

"I think … I think company, too," Keiko whispered back. "Because they are all here still, and they have no more class today."

"Who do you think will get Sugarplum?" continued Taylor, as they went downstairs. "Oh, and where were you yesterday?!"

"I was at home. I had jetlag still," said Keiko. "I think maybe Alexandra, but also maybe Grace? Because the Demidovskis really like Grace. But I like Alexandra is better, I think she is a better dancer. And maybe Anna for something, but I don't know what." They got changed, and Taylor drank a ROCKSTAR. Taylor walked into Studio A. *F,* she thought. *Tristan's taken my favourite spot on barre again.*

"Hey, Gaylor, 'sup?" Tristan called across the room. Everyone started giggling.

"You're almost too gay to function," she said, trying not to cry.

"Oh, quoting *Mean Girls*? Were you in that?" he laughed.

Delilah started laughing even harder, "Didn't you know? She was the stupid blonde one."

Taylor went to the back *barre*, forcing herself to giggle, and said, "It's not nice to make fun of me just 'cause I'm blonde!" Keiko was at the back *barre* too. "Hey, Keiko. *O-genki desuka?*"

"*Hai, genki desu,*" replied Keiko smiling. "Your Japanese is improving!" Keiko frowned as Kaitlyn walked in. "Who is that?"

"Kaitlyn," whispered Taylor. "She's really good. She wins, like, everything and she gets hundreds in her exams."

"Oh." Keiko didn't look very happy. "Well, she does not have a good body type."

"No, I know, "said Taylor, agreeing happily. "Who do we have for warm-up class?"

"Mr. Yu," answered Angela from behind them.

"Oh, great," said Keiko to Taylor, ignoring Angela. "I haven't had a Mr. Yu class for a while."

Mr. Yu came in and scowled at the class. Standing in the doorway, he slowly scanned the room. His eyes rested on Taylor. "Where is your uniform?"

"S-s-sorry," stuttered Taylor. "I thought, because, like we don't have to wear a uniform for the audition, that, maybe ... we didn't have to wear uniform for class...." Her voice got quieter and quieter until nobody but Keiko could hear the last few words.

"Wazzat you say?" demanded Mr. Yu, cupping his hand around his ear.

Anna called out, "She said that she thought we didn't have to wear uniform today because we don't have to for the audition class."

Mr. Yu gestured at Anna to shut up, saying, "Can she speak English? She doesn't look Japanese. Does she need a translator maybe? Come on, speak."

Taylor tried again. "I thought we didn't need to wear uniform today...."

"What's that?!" said Mr. Yu, raising his eyebrows in disbelief. "Is this class?"

"Yes, but ..." Taylor tried to shrink into the *barre*.

"No but! Is this class?"

"Yes."

"Look around," said Mr. Yu, gesturing around the room. "You see anyone else not wear uniform?"

"No," whispered Taylor.

"What did you say?" asked Mr. Yu. "No, right? Everyone have the little VIBA on hip?" he said, poking Keiko's hip where the academy's logo was embroidered on her bodysuit. "Don't even need to read, just look.

Oh, white spot? Must be VIBA, right?" Taylor nodded. Suddenly his smile disappeared and he looked furious. "Next time, no uniform, no class. I will kick you out. Understand?" Without waiting for an answer he began to lead class.

The class collectively began to breathe again, those around Taylor staring at her with alternating expressions of pity and disgust.

"And into, *hu, ha, phu, ba, ba, chuuuu ... pah! Ba,* into ..." Mr. Yu called out the counts for each exercise in his own peculiar way while banging the Nutcracker Prince's prop sword in time to the music to make more noise. George gritted his teeth and tried to block him out by hitting the keys louder. *WHAP!* "*Into...!*" bellowed Mr. Yu, hitting Julian on his leg with the sword while he was in arabesque. Julian grimaced in pain and squared his hips. "Okay, *barre* finish. Now stretch," said Mr. Yu, finally. He went out for a smoke.

Taylor sat on the ground and rolled into the middle splits. Julian came over and slid into the side splits next to her. "Hey, you okay?" he asked. "That dude is kinda intense."

"Yeah, I know. It's just Mr. Yu, he's like that," Taylor was trying not to cry. Angela came and sat down beside them.

"Taylor, how come you didn't just wear your uniform?" she asked in a fake-friendly tone. "It says in the rule book to *always* wear the uniform for class," she added condescendingly. Taylor said nothing.

Julian stared at her like she was crazy. "Wow, you're really rude, you know that? Why don't you F off?"

"I was trying to make her feel better!" said Angela, moving away horrified. Taylor started laughing.

"That was good," she turned to Julian. "Thanks! She's, like, always a bitch to me."

"No problem," he said "Anyway, she is so bad! I couldn't stop laughing at her yesterday while I was sitting out. And she thinks she's really good!" Tristan came over and sat next to Julian. Delilah followed him, and Taylor quickly got up and left.

"Did you just tell Angela to F off?" he asked, grinning at Julian.

"Ah, yeah. But she was being really rude." he started to try to justify himself.

"Hey, no, that's cool!" Tristan said, "I've totally wanted to do that since she came, just couldn't find an excuse."

"I gave you loads!" complained Delilah.

"So," said Tristan, ignoring Delilah, "we were wondering if you'd been to Harbour Dance yet?"

"No, what's that?" asked Julian.

"It's this dance place. It's really cool. They have drop-in classes running all day, every day, and all types, and you just pay per class. It's really awesome for contemporary and hip hop and stuff. It's not like they have any good contemporary at the academy. You should totally come with us some day."

"I'd like that," smiled Julian.

"Right, see you then, Jules," said Tristan. At that moment Mr. Yu came back, looking distinctly calmer from the smoke.

"The more you smoke, the more you jump," he told Alexandra, who was sitting off to the side with a stomach ache, as he walked in. "Everyone, centre," he called out.

"I'm nervous," Taylor whispered to Kaitlyn as they waited for the auditions.

"Why?" asked Kaitlyn, snorting. "It's not like we dance, right? Delilah said that we just stand in order of height and they pick."

"Yes, but, like, I'm not like *really* nervous. I just want to do well," said Taylor, quickly editing.

"Right," Kaitlyn rolled her eyes. Mr. and Mrs. Demidovski came in, and everyone slowly quieted down.

Mr. Demidovski was wearing black dress pants, a white dress shirt with the sleeves rolled up, a black vest, black dress shoes, and a green cloak with a multicoloured plaid lining. On top of all this, he had added a gold scarf.

"I like your scarf, Mr. Demidovski," Tristan said, grinning.

"Thank you," Mr. Demidovski inclined his head toward Tristan and bowed slightly. "And how are you?"

"Good, sir," Tristan bit his finger to keep himself from laughing out loud.

"Okay, everyone line up, smallest to tallest," yelled Mr. Yu.

Mr. Moretti stood to one side watching the proceedings balefully. He sighed, and then walked to the front where Mrs. Demidovski, Mrs. Castillo, and Mrs. Mallard were already sitting. Mr. Damon, the artistic director of the youth company, was also there. After due consideration, Mr. Moretti sat down next to Mr. Damon, evidently judging him to be the lesser of the evils. Mr. Demidovski walked to the front of the room and surveyed his students proudly.

"Today ... today we have the audition," he announced proudly. "We have auditions for *The Nutcracker*. My academy, it is going to perform *The Nutcracker* for the Christmas show. Today, we pick the parts of Clara and Sugarplum. Everyone, I do not want you to cry. I do not want you tell your parents that it is not fair. Mr. Demidovski is a very fair man, everyone says that. Everyone. All the parts are important. All take work; all are important for a beautiful show. Mr. Yu, would you like to say anything to the students?" Mr. Yu shook his head. He was standing next to Tristan with his hands in his pockets, waiting impatiently. When Mr. Demidovski turned away from Mr. Yu, Tristan gave a snort of smothered laughter, and Mr. Yu hit him on the ear. "All right, we start!" announced Mr. Demidovski. "Everybody stand tallest to smallest? Okay." He turned to Mrs. Demidovski and whispered in Russian.

"Yes, Alexandra is here," said Mrs. Demidovski loudly in English.

Alexandra rolled her eyes. "Good thing he knows what I look like, hey?" she whispered to Grace. Grace gave a small smile and kept her eyes facing front.

"Grace, come front," said Mr. Yu.

"Okay, so she's first cast Sugarplum." Taylor whispered to Keiko, keeping her eyes on Mr. Yu.

"So if they know what we're cast as, we get called up front?" Julian whispered to Tristan.

"No." replied Tristan. "Principals get called front, solos and good corps to the side, and losers to the back. Pretty simple, really. They don't even tell you what you got until rehearsals next week. Not that they have to, we know."

"Aiko, Kaitlyn ... Anna ... Michael ..." continued Mr. Yu. Taylor's stomach dropped. *Not Kaitlyn! She just got here, does she have to get Clara? It had to be Clara! She's the only one short enough to dance Clara. At least they aren't using the professional company members this year.*

Mr. Demidovski called Mr. Yu over and they had a quickly whispered discussion. "Okay, Alexandra!" called Mr. Yu, not making any pretence of being happy about it. "Julie!" Julian got up as everyone in the room laughed nervously. "And Tristan, Kageki, Jonathon. Are we using Dmitri?" he asked Mr. Damon, who nodded.

"Okay," Mr. Yu said, suddenly speeding up, running through the lists of names as he sent them to the sides and back. "Okay, finish." He went and crouched down beside Mr. Demidovski. "Good?"

"Yes. Thank you, Mr. Yu. Everyone, you may go. Rehearsal on Saturday. Look on the board. If anyone's name wasn't called, go talk to Gabriel in the office." Everyone clapped and filed silently out of the room, except Taylor who was chattering excitedly to Keiko.

"Keiko, I'm so happy!" she said, grabbing onto Keiko's arm as they walked out. "This is the first year I'm not in like Russian or Arabian, or something stupid. Do you think I'm in Snow? Or Waltz of Flowers? I'm so happy."

"That's good," said Keiko as they went downstairs. She didn't look terribly happy herself. "I wonder what

Chloe got," she said as they walked into the washroom. "She can't be Clara, she's too young! But she can't be anything else either."

Anna joined in, "Yeah, I know, it's stupid. At first I thought Kaitlyn got Clara, but then they called up Chloe. Maybe they're double cast? But Chloe would look better as Clara, her body type is better." said Anna thoughtfully.

"Yes, she would look better," said Keiko. "Yes, maybe it would be good, and she would look nice with Michael as Fritz."

"Yes," Anna agreed. They went to join the lineup for the washroom stalls, having reached their verdict.

"Hey, Taylor, what did *you* get?" Kaitlyn asked condescendingly as they opened their lockers. Taylor deflated.

"Um, I'm not sure..." she said unhappily. "I think probably, like, Waltz of Flowers or Snow? I'm not really sure."

"Oh, yeah, I liked those parts," laughed Kaitlyn. "I was both two years ago for second cast, it was fun. But I was Clara for first cast, so I couldn't do both. Last year I was Sugarplum, though, so I didn't have time to do Waltz and Snow as well. You'll like it, it's lots of fun!" she laughed. Taylor didn't say anything; she just went and got dressed. She felt sick.

As Taylor walked down the hall to leave, Mrs. Demidovski stopped her. "Taylor!" she said. "Come into office, Mrs. Demidovski wants to talk to you."

Taylor followed her into the office apprehensively. It was empty except for Gabriel, who was doing paperwork and eating Smarties.

"Come, come, sit down. Your mother, she phoned Mrs. Demidosvksi. She said that you want to take RAD Advanced One exam this spring."

"Yes," said Taylor, wishing that she was anywhere but that office.

"Mrs. Demidovski think you are not ready. I think maybe get stronger, need more muscle. Body good," she grabbed Taylor's arm and wrapped her fingers around Taylor's wrist to check how much they crossed over. "But you need more strength. You need to work harder. If 'push,' push; if 'straight,' straight."

"Okay," said Taylor, wanting to leave. Mrs. Demidovski looked at her over her glass of water.

"So, you will take the exam next year?" she asked, her eyes amused.

"I would … I mean, I would really like, to you know, take the exam this year." Taylor said, pleading.

"If you take the exam, you must take privates. Arrange it with Gabriel tomorrow, talk to your mother tomorrow."

"Okay!" Taylor was relieved. She got up to leave.

"Good girl," said Mrs. Demidovski, smiling up at her. "Much improve. Don't worry." Taylor smiled back and left happily.

As she went to catch the bus to the SkyTrain, Taylor noticed that Delilah, Tristan, and Julian were already there waiting. She quickly turned back before they saw her. She decided to take the next bus and walked over to Duan's to get a bubble tea. She waited patiently to order. Duan's was a wonderful world of white flour, liquid sugar, and suspicious meat, and they made the sweetest all-fruit bubble tea in Vancouver. Taylor ordered the mango and papaya milk tea with pearls, and watched as Mrs. Duan ladled the liquid sugar in. She carefully selected her straw (*hot pink today, I think*), which was extra large to let the pearls through, and checked which cartoon character was on the plastic covering before she stuck her straw through it. It was some sort of cross between a skunk and a monkey. She drank her bubble tea slowly, feeling happier as she drank. A bubble tea always made her feel better.

As Taylor walked slowly back to the bus stop, a druggie started calling to her. "Hey you! Hey you, you look single! Come here!" Taylor broke into a run and reached the bus stop before she had intended to. She checked her bubble tea; none had spilled. As the bus pulled up, she entered through the rear doors, just in case the bus driver decided to enforce the no-eating-or-drinking policy. Taking out her iPod, she relaxed into her seat, drowning out the sounds of the boy sitting next to her talking on his cell with "Ur So Gay" by Katy Perry. She couldn't help it, every time she listened to the lyrics, "You're so gay and you don't even *like* boys," she had to giggle. Getting bored, she decided to call Kaitlyn as she got off the bus. Kaitlyn probably hadn't *meant* to be mean about casting, she convinced herself. It was just that she was always cast in good roles, because she was so good. She got Kaitlyn's answering machine, and decided to leave her a message.

"Hey.... So I'm about to get on the SkyTrain. And I decided to phone you, because I am, like, sooooo bored.

Are you going to be at school tomorrow? Well, yeah, you probably will, because, like, why wouldn't you be?" Taylor looked around her and stage whispered, "Okay, so I am feeling a *little* grossed out right now. There is this person, and she is like *huge*. I really wish you were here with me to see! So, anyway, I really hope you can come to my party on Friday. It's going to be lots of fun. Remember to wear a dress, we are all going to take *so* many pictures, it'll be awesome. So, the SkyTrain is coming in now, you can probably hear it!" Taylor giggled, "So I'll see you tomorrow. Bye, love you!" Taylor hung up and got on the SkyTrain, having completely forgotten both Mr. Yu's rant and that Kaitlyn had been cast ahead of her. The academy always seemed unreal to Taylor once she had left the building.

Walking into her house, Taylor suddenly felt less exuberant. She remembered that she had hidden a tube of ready-made icing in her room. Squirting some into her mouth, she then stuffed the tube back into a pair of folded socks. She felt better. "Mom, I'm home!" she called out.

"Oh, hi, baby. How was it?" Charlize came into her room and sat on the bed.

"Um ..." said Taylor, quickly searching her brain for what "it" was. "Oh! It was good. I think I got Waltz or Snow, I was put on the side and was one of the first called."

"That's good." Charlize sounded relieved. "What did Kaitlyn get?"

"Um, I think Clara," said Taylor quietly.

Charlize just sighed.

"Mom!" said Taylor angrily. "Look, Waltz or Snow is really good, okay? Can you just leave it, please? Why do you always have to *do* this?" She was trying not to cry.

"Taylor, I'm not saying —" Charlize started, but Taylor ran out of the room and went and sat on the stairs until her mom had left her room.

Back in her room, Taylor logged onto her laptop. *There's something I wanted to do ... Oh, add that new boy! What was his name?* She checked her newsfeed on Facebook. Tristan had just added a Julian Reese. *Right, that's him.* She clicked on friend request. Just then, her little sister, Alison, came to the door.

"Hey," she said, fidgeting.

"What are you doing?" Alison had something hidden behind her back. "Alison, if you don't want to say anything get out of here. I'm busy." Alison came in and sat down.

"Look at this, "she said proudly. From behind her back she produced a test paper. She walked in and sat down on the bed next to Taylor. "See: 100 percent!"

"Oh ... good job," Taylor said unenthusiastically. Seeing Alison's face fall, she added, "That's really great! I can't believe you got perfect on a math test, that's, like, awesome, Ali." Alison smiled proudly.

As Taylor got into bed and took her sleeping pill, she thought about her party. She wondered if she would get a chance to invite Julian (*Jules,* she remembered) to the party. He seemed really nice. *I wonder if he was straight.* She frowned slightly as she fell asleep, worrying about Tristan and Delilah. *Maybe they won't like Jules,* she thought hopefully.

Chapter Three

Alexandra Dunstan
Genee was so much fun, I love you all!!! Never forget...

Alexandra walked out of the academy. She felt numb. She aimed for her dad's car, trying to walk normally. She pasted a smile on her face as she passed all the other students leaving. Seeing her face, Peter Dunstan pulled out as soon as she had closed the door, leaving the academy as quickly as he could. As soon as she was sure they were out of sight, Alexandra burst into tears.

"What happened?" Peter Dunstan asked sympathetically, while trying to manoeuvre into the fast lane.

"They ... they did it again!" sobbed Alexandra. "I'm double cast with Anna for *Arabian*! And Grace and Aiko are sharing Sugarplum and Snow Queen, and Anna's also sharing Rose Queen with the new girl, Kaitlyn! She's already got one cast of Clara. I can't believe the Demidovskis did this again! I am so F-ing sick of it! *And* Leon and Jonathon are the slave boys!"

"How do you know what you got already? I thought they only told you on Saturday?"

"Oh, well this year we have to sign a contract." Alexandra wiped her eyes and checked her eyeliner in the mirror. "Everybody who got a principal or solo role had to. So we all said we weren't going to sign if they didn't tell us what we got." Peter Dunstan raised his eyebrows. "Okay," Alexandra smiled slightly. "Tristan said that, and then we all sort of nodded in agreement. I mean, they can't kick Tristan out, they don't have enough boys in the academy to do that. And none of the boys in the company would do it for free. They're already paying Dmitri to do Cavalier. They're not exactly going to pay another boy."

"Lexi, it's actually okay that you only got Arabian. You sat out yesterday because of your stomach, right?"

"Yes."

"Well, we'll just tell everyone that you needed some rest because of Genee, so you asked the Demidovskis to give you something less demanding for *The Nutcracker*. We can say that we wanted to take you away for a vacation to recover, and just skip *The Nutcracker* altogether, but the Demidovskis begged you to stay, and we just couldn't let them down. Since you got bronze, everyone will believe that," he nodded to himself, satisfied.

"Dad, that's perfect!" said Alexandra, much happier. Blowing her nose one last time, she reached to turn on the music.

"Lexi, do you have to turn that on right now?" Peter groaned.

"Yes. I *could* use my iPod, but then I would be destroying my ears ..." she said, raising her eyebrows.

"Fine then, but no Damien Rice, or Radiohead, or Coldplay."

"Dad, fine! I'll put on Kelly Clarkson!"

"Great! I like her songs ... I think."

Alexandra rolled her eyes.

As they walked in the door, Beth Dunstan called out, "Good, you're here! The meat's just done, perfect timing!"

"Mom, I told you, I'm going vegetarian," Alexandra said, frowning as she walked into the kitchen.

"Well, the rest of the family isn't, sweetie." Beth gave Alexandra a hug. "And you're too skinny right now. It was fine for Genee, but you don't need it for now. I don't want you going to McKinley looking like a concentration-camp prisoner. I don't appreciate all the phone calls from 'concerned counsellors.'"

"Mom! Could you please just *not!*"

"Okay, okay. How was the academy today?" Beth mashed the potatoes.

"I didn't get a good part. Only one cast of Arabian lead, and Grace got Sugarplum first cast *and* Snow Queen second cast, but it's okay," Alexandra peeled a mandarin orange. "Dad said we can just tell everyone I needed a break because of Genee."

"That's a good idea. I'm sorry about that, though, honey. I thought things would be different with a bronze. Oh, well. Could you please call your sister and brother down for dinner?"

"Sure," said Alexandra. Going upstairs, she called, "Justin! Emma! Dinnertime!"

She went into her room and closed the door. Trying to breathe normally and calm down, she sat on her bed. *Why does this always have to happen?* Alexandra thought miserably. *Why couldn't they just cast me? No, every time, I have to stand in that stupid line, and watch, as people who aren't as good as me get cast above me, yet again. Don't cry, don't eat, don't hyperventilate,* she willed herself to calm down, silently. Grabbing her knees, Alexandra hunched herself into a ball. She stared down at her feet. *Great,* she thought, *that blister has gotten even bigger. I wonder if I should wear the stupid Gaynor Mindens tomorrow to give it a better chance to recover.* As casting suddenly came back to her mind, Alexandra's legs flew out from under her elbows. She scrunched her eyes shut, trying to drive the image away.

Alexandra lay under her blankets. *It's midnight, go to sleep,* she thought. Giving up, she got out of bed and sat down at the computer, staring blearily at the screen. She checked Facebook: one friend request. Clicking on it, she frowned. *Julian Reese, who on earth is that? Oh, the new boy,* she remembered. She clicked accept. Finding an old *Skins* episode, and plugging in her headphones so she didn't wake anyone else up, she sat down on the chair and sighed, resigning herself to a long night.

At breakfast the next morning, Alexandra was not at all tired. From past experience, she knew that this meant she would suddenly run out of adrenalin in the middle of ballet class. Justin was at the counter making what appeared to be a lot of sandwiches. "Are you making some for me and Emma, too?" Alexandra asked Justin suspiciously.

"Yeah right! Make your own," Justin said. "I'm staying late at UBC and I want to watch a soccer match, so I need extra sustenance."

"Why don't you actually play yourself?" Alexandra asked as she inspected the fruit bowl.

"It's a *girl's* team, *duh*," Justin rolled his eyes.

"Where's Emma? And Mom and Dad?" Alexandra had suddenly noticed the absence of half her family.

"Dad's at work, and Mom's with Emma at some gymnastics meet. Your friend Grace's mom is coming by to pick you up for school. In, like, half an hour I think.... I dunno, I wasn't really listening."

"Oh *great*," groaned Alexandra. The last thing she felt like doing was taking an almost hour-long car ride with Grace and her mother.

As Alexandra got in the car, April Kendall said, "Oh Lexi, sweetie, we all missed you so much! I haven't seen that beautiful face in so long! You aren't looking very well, though, honey. I was just telling Grace that. I do hope you aren't ill!"

"No, I'm just fine, April!" said Alexandra, smiling through gritted teeth. Grace smiled sympathetically at her, and Alexandra remembered why she actually did like Grace sometimes, like when it wasn't casting day.

"Hey, Mom, wait a sec, 'kay?" said Grace. "I'm going to go sit in the back with Lexi."

"Of course, darling. You probably have to tell Lexi all about what has been going on here while she's been away!

And let me tell you, sweetie," she turned around in her seat so she could see Alexandra, "there has been a *lot* going on." Alexandra smiled sickly a sweet smile back at her.

Everybody actually made it to the bus stop after school on time for the first bus.

"Wow, even Leon made it," laughed Tristan as they filed on the bus. It was same bus driver as the day before, and recognizing him, Tristan laughed. "Hey, 'sup?" he asked, grinning.

The bus driver looked at him sourly. "Have you lot multiplied?" he asked suspiciously.

"No. Maybe you're seeing things," Tristan asked earnestly, peering up at him with a concerned expression on his face.

Looking nervously at an old lady sitting in one of the front seats who looked distinctly worried, the bus driver growled, "No, get back there." He gestured towards the back.

Julian giggled as he followed Tristan to the back seats. Kaitlyn pushed past Taylor to sit next to the boys and Delilah, and Taylor quickly took the last back seat, cutting out Jessica. Everyone else scattered around the bus, trying to get good seats. Alexandra and Grace ignored them all and sat at the front, next the old lady.

"If anyone asks, we just look young for our age and have mental problems," Grace whispered in Alexandra's ear. Alexandra gave a snort and collapsed into giggles, worrying the old lady again. She got up and slowly walked to the door.

"I don't like teenagers," she loudly told the bus driver as he lowered the ramp for her to get off. He smiled sympathetically.

"Who do we have today?" Alexandra asked Grace as they walked into the academy.

"Um…" Grace checked her schedule. "Mr. Yu for ballet again, and then some contemporary class. It's a new teacher again, I don't recognize the initials."

Alexandra peered at the board and frowned. "SP? I don't know any contemporary teacher with those initials. Oh well, maybe it will be good."

"*Maybe,*" a voice said from behind them.

"Yeah, you're right, Kageki," laughed Alexandra. "*Maybe.* So," Taylor was standing nearby. "Go away! So, Grace, do you want to go shopping after this?"

"Um … okay," Grace was unenthusiastic. "But Anna has to come too. I kind of told her we would hang out today."

"Anna?" Alexandra said disgustedly. "Why her? Okay, okay, we'll all go." She grabbed her uniform and went to get changed.

Up in the studio, Alexandra went to the center *barre*, mirror side, Mao and Jessica quickly moving to make room for her.

"Aww, Lexi, I missed you baby!" said Tristan, smirking at her.

"Missed you toooo, honey sugar," she said matching his tone and smiling at him.

"Come, I'll stretch your feet if you tell me how it was, Miss Bronze!" Tristan rolled over to her. "Did you find any hot guys?"

"No, the only straight one was five feet tall and didn't speak English," Alexandra sighed, sticking out her feet to be stretched.

"Well, were there any hot ones that were sort of bent? Slightly curvy?" Tristan asked, giggling up at her. "God, your feet are like rocks. My arms are in pain!"

"Ow!" Alexandra groaned. "Um, there was one that was, like, almost a full circle, but he was really good looking. He got to finals, but didn't win anything. I added him on Facebook, so I can show you later if you want." Mr. Yu walked into the room grinning happily. "This is going to be a good class!" Alexandra whispered excitedly to everyone in the general vicinity.

Mr. Yu walked over to the *barre* and bent over backwards on it, cracking his back. Swinging his arms violently, and then pushing his hips out towards all four corners of the room, he proceeded to pop and crack every part of his body. Finished, he began stretching his hamstrings and said, "Before you take class, you should crack everything."

"Uh oh," groaned Tristan to Delilah. "I think this is gonna be a lecture day."

Mr. Yu continued, "Ballet dancing is the hardest sport. It is not just a sport, because it is art. That makes it double, triple times harder. And ballet dancers need to be smart," he tapped his head. "Cannot be stupid. Actually, ballet makes you smarter. That is why you need to work double, triple times. Stretching when you warm ... not as good as when cold. If you want to be flexible, you should stretch when you first wake up, before you go to school, when the body is cold."

"I think that goes against what every other fitness instructor and physiotherapist in the world would say," Julian whispered to Tristan.

"Wait, it gets better," Tristan said gleefully.

"At Beijing Ballet Academy, we would run in the park. At maybe 5:30 or 6:30. First run, then run with jumps, all through the park. After this, we would stretch on trees," Mr. Yu continued, sticking his leg on the bar and bending his body over his leg to demonstrate how they stretched.

"I can't believe he can still do that," Julian whispered in astonishment, as Mr. Yu pulled his toes till they rested under his chin, his whole body lying flat on his leg.

"He keeps flexible by showing off for us," Tristan said cynically.

"Canadians are wasteful," said Mr. Yu, suddenly changing the topic. "In China, nothing is wasted. Even hair is sold. You die, hair sold. Make stuff like the eyelashes you wear for performance."

"Ewww!" the class groaned in unison. Mr. Yu looked pleased with himself, having achieved the effect he wanted.

"You mean when it says 'real hair' on the fake eyelash box they mean it? And it comes off of *dead people*?" Alexandra asked horrified. Mr. Yu nodded. "Gross!"

"Okay, *pliés*," said Mr. Yu, satisfied. He taught a very exhausting class, and everyone left the room groaning and complaining about their various body parts. Alexandra beamed happily as she left: a good hard class was exactly what she'd needed.

They moved languidly as they added layers, rolled up tights and pants, and took down their hair for contemporary class. The class took little interest in the contemporary teacher. She was wearing Lululemon pants and looked like almost every other contemporary teacher, not a ballet teacher.

Mrs. Demidovski walked into the studio, her heels clicking firmly on the floor. "Hello," she said, staring around at the class. Almost a quarter of the students were missing. "Where are the rest of the students?" No one answered. Angela put up her hand, but Mrs. Demidovski ignored her. "Tristan! Come here." Tristan obeyed. "Sit down," The class immediately fell to the floor, happy for the break. Tristan dropped to the ground right in front of Mrs. Demidovski and folded his long legs into a cross-legged position. "Tristan," she asked. "Where is everyone?"

"I don't know," he put a sincere expression on his face. "Maybe they are sick?"

Angela rocked back and forth, whispering urgently to Jessica, "They're not sick, they're skipping! Just because its contemporary doesn't mean they can skip!"

"Quiet, please!" Mrs. Demidovski sounded irritated. "It's okay, it's okay …" she gestured at Tristan to move back again. He scooted back on his butt, coming to a halt between Delilah and Julian. Coughing, Mrs. Demidovski introduced the new teacher. "This is … *Sukuuuya. Sukuuuya* Paulen."

"Actually," corrected the contemporary teacher, smiling sweetly, "it's Sequoia."

"Oh god, another freak," Alexandra whispered to Anna.

"I, like, *need* to meditate right now," answered Anna, sighing. "I can't move." Mrs. Demidovski frowned at the girls.

"Yes, *Sukuuuya*," Mrs. Demidovski said firmly. "*Sukuuuya* is a very good teacher. She teaches all over world. Everybody likes her very much. I want everyone to take the contemporary class, and work hard. Maybe those who do not have good feet, too tall, too this, too that," she mimed huge boobs, "you can do contemporary. Many things not okay for ballet, okay in contemporary. You try. See?" she said gesturing at Sequoia. "She maybe not have so good body for ballet, no good feet, try contemporary. Possible okay." Sequoia looked at her, her vague expression focusing into an expression of sadness for the unenlightened. Looking rather uncomfortable, Mrs. Demidovski started to leave, saying, "Tristan, you tell all boys must come to contemporary class! De-Li-Lah, you tell girls."

"Class, I am so happy that we have this opportunity to get to know each other," said Sequoia. "I want everyone to just scatter around the floor, but not too far. If you have something on your feet, I want you to take it off," Alexandra groaned. Now she knew her blister was going to get infected for sure. "Take your hair down if it is still up. I want you to be able to feel it swing and lead you."

"Eww," Alexandra complained to Anna, "my hair is all sweaty and gross. And the gel isn't helping."

Kaitlyn was at the front. She kept her eyes on the teacher, nodding after everything she said.

"Do you believe that?" Anna whispered to Alexandra, pointed at Kaitlyn.

"Mphh," Alexandra muttered, not paying attention and trying to smooth her hair down in the mirror.

"Everyone, just walk," said Sequoia. "Let your arms swing, and breathe normally. Walk at a steady pace, pick a path and keep on that path, but do not walk into anyone.... Now, speed up, and move closer to each other. Yes, weaving *in* and *out*, through each other, tighter.... Now, make eye contact with the person directly in front of you, keep moving towards them. When you are almost touching, stop. Follow that person's movements, take turns leading. Do not move your feet. Focus on your upper body. Notice your partner's breathing and try to match it, become one body.... Okay, everyone, come and sit down in a circle."

"Do you think she'll put on any music anytime during this class?" Alexandra whispered to Grace.

"I don't know," Grace whispered back, "but I'm totally going to go crazy if she doesn't."

"Now lie on your backs, close your eyes, and *breathe*," Sequoia continued. "I want you to imagine that you are walking in a beautiful forest. Imagine how it feels, and find peace in your enjoyment of this forest. Let your arms rest loosely at your sides, and let your lower back find a comfortable position. Now start rocking *up* and *down*, starting the motion from your heels. Yes, that's right." Standing over Kaitlyn, she asked, "What's your name?"

"Kaitlyn," she said, smiling up at Sequoia smugly.

"Very good, Kaitlyn!"

Anna pushed her heels violently into the floor, sending her body to the side by accident. "Careful, careful. Not too vigorously, now," Sequoia cautioned. After the rocking exercise, they slowly progressed to floor work.

During a "just move across the floor concentrating on your feet, don't hurry, move at your own pace" exercise, Alexandra looked at the clock for the twentieth time and noticed that the hands had actually moved. "Look!" she whispered excitedly to Tristan. "We're finished soon!"

"Thank god," Tristan whispered back. "I was *that* close to just running out the door when she was telling me to just '*be* the deer'!"

"Everyone, come and sit down," said Sequoia. "Let your breath slowly return."

"We weren't doing anything! My breath is intact!" Alexandra complained to Tristan.

"Please do not to talk during class," Sequoia said, a slight frown creasing her brow. "It is disrespectful to your classmates. Now, I believe that in order to become a successful dancer, you must know yourself. When I say successful dancer, I do *not* mean one that is successful in the eyes of teachers or judges. I mean someone who knows themselves so completely, that they can *transcend* their body to connect with an audience. To be able to accomplish this is to be a truly great dancer. When you dance, you should feel *goosebumps* on your arms. It is only when you have really come out of yourself that you have *truly* experienced what it is to dance." Alexandra tried to smother a yawn. "During this class, I feel that I have really been able to get to know the *real* you, so I am going to attempt to act as a mirror, and show you bits of yourself that you may not have known before. What's your name?" Sequoia asked Tristan.

"Ah ... Tristan?"

"Now, that's interesting, Tristan. Did you notice that you just said your name as a question? Are you quite sure that your name is Tristan?"

"Yes, my name is Tristan," Tristan said, a bit confused and annoyed.

"That's much better, Tristan! Now, Tristan, I want you to just close your eyes and think. I want you to imagine that a fly is coming to rest on your head. Swat it away. Good, good, that's very good. Now stand up ... and then put all your weight on one leg. Good! You can open your eyes now."

"Great," Tristan answered sarcastically.

"Now, Tristan," Sequoia said with an understanding smile, "if you were angry with me right now, would you most want to punch me or call me names?"

"Call you names," Tristan answered without hesitation. Delilah giggled.

"Ah, I think you are not in touch enough with your masculine side. You are really going to have to work on that to become more well-rounded." Tristan looked at her in disbelief, and everyone started to giggle. "Might I suggest maybe focusing on some pursuits that bring out your manly side?" Sequoia was apparently oblivious to the class's reaction. "Maybe try some baseball or soccer … you know, even just doing some extra math might help."

Alexandra raised her hand to her mouth, trying not to laugh.

"Oh my God, do you believe that woman?" Tristan said angrily as they walked down the stairs after class. "Like, does she even know what gay *means*?"

"No, I don't think she does," Alexandra laughed.

"Even I know what gay means, and I'm Japanese," Kageki said in disgust.

"I am *so* not taking that class again," Tristan jumped into the lost and found bin. Taking a lost doll out, he held in front of his face. "I think you need to get in touch with your *masculine* side," he said in a high-pitched voice, imitating Sequoia.

"And Mrs. Demidovski said we had to tell everyone to come to this class." Delilah shook her head scornfully. "As if!"

"Yeah! Yeah right!" Tristan stuffed the doll violently back in the lost and found.

"Hey, Tristan," said Alexandra, doing up her shoes, "do you want to come with Grace, Anna, and me? We're going shopping."

"Where?" Tristan brightened up.

"Robson, duh!"

"That sounds like fun …" Delilah hinted. Alexandra and Tristan ignored her.

"Oh, Lexi," Grace said, "I think I'm actually going to just go home? I'm kind of tired. Anna, we can still hang out though, if you want. We've been planning this for such a long time. Do you want to come sleep over?"

"Sure," Anna grinned at Alexandra.

"Well, do you still want to go?" Alexandra asked Tristan, trying to keep the anger out of her voice. Glancing over at Delilah, Alexandra added, "You can come, too, if you want."

"Sure!" Delilah said happily.

"That sounds fun," Tristan smirked at Alexandra, who was watching Grace and Anna leave. She looked nauseated.

"So, what's the new guy like?" Alexandra asked as they waited for the bus. She suddenly remembered how little sleep she had gotten the night before, and yawned.

"Oh, Jules? He's really cool, and nice," said Tristan enthusiastically. Alexandra looked at him sharply. "He homestays at Mr. Yu's. I went over there yesterday. We had a lot of fun, except it was laundry day, so nobody was supposed to come over. I tried hiding in Keiko 's closet every time Mr. Yu came by, 'cause me, Jules, and Keiko were playing cards in her room, but then he heard my voice, and he was like '*Wazzat? Who there?*' and so he gave me a lecture and hit me with the broom. It was fun though."

"Jules sounds nice," Alexandra said neutrally. "He seems straight, is he?"

"Oh, I don't know."

"He is *definitely* straight," Delilah said, giggling. "He couldn't be that clueless and be gay." Tristan glared at her, annoyed.

"Some people are gay and clueless," he said. "And it's okay that he's clueless, because he's kind of smart."

"It doesn't really matter, right?" Alexandra said firmly as they got on the bus. "Where do you want to go first? We don't have loads of time."

"Zara," said Tristan. "No, wait, H&M. It's closer if we're taking this bus."

"'Kay," said Alexandra. "Sounds good to me."

"Yeah, me too," said Delilah. "But can we stop by the gelato place after? I'm starving."

"Sure. I haven't been there in a long time," said Alexandra. They got off the bus and started walking to H&M. "I love being downtown at this time of day. It's so happy, you know? Full of tourists who just had a long day and are wandering around relaxing, and the druggies haven't come out in full force yet."

"Yeah, okay, Lexi," Tristan said, laughing. "But no, you're right, it is nice wandering around down here this time of day."

"Um, yeah," said Delilah, staring in disgust at a man who was relieving himself in an alley. "It kind of depends on *where* downtown, don'tcha think? Like, more there than here," she pointed up the street to where H&M was and walked quickly. Tristan and Alexandra laughed and followed her.

Later, as they walked into Mondo Gelato, Tristan and Delilah were arguing. "I just don't like them, okay?" Tristan said firmly.

"Why?" demanded Delilah. "Look, they are sooooo cute!"

"I don't like the shoes. They're ugly," repeated Tristan for the third time.

Ignoring them both, Alexandra went up to the counter and looked. Half blueberry sorbet, half pine-apple, she decided. That was what she always got.

"May I try the strawberry sorbet?" Alexandra asked the server. "And then the mango, and then the mint? Thanks.... Actually, can I have one scoop in a cup, half blueberry sorbet, half..." *Oh why not be different for once,* she thought recklessly, "banana sorbet?"

"Sure," the server said, laughing slightly.

"It's a gelato place," Delilah said when they all had their orders and were sitting at a table outside. "How come you two both ordered sorbet?"

"It's better for you. It has less calories," Alexandra and Tristan answered at the same time.

"Jinx, give me a Coca-Cola!" Alexandra laughed. They finished their desserts slowly as it got dark, and then started walking back down Robson.

"Oh, look, it's the mime dude!" Delilah said excitedly.

"Delilah, that guy is here all the time, we can watch another day," Alexandra said, stopping to watch none-theless. They laughed as a Japanese tourist jumped back — the mime was pretending to try and kiss her. Then he turned around and had a fake fight with her boyfriend, who couldn't stop laughing.

"Okay, we totally have to go, like, now," said Tristan. "Lexi, is your mom picking you up?"

"No, my dad. I phoned him while you two were arguing over the shoes. He's going to meet me in front of Le Château and Bebe. Do you need a ride?"

"Yes, please."

"I can bus," Delilah said, but Alexandra ignored her.

"Good, that's fine then," Tristan answered for her.

"Hey, Tristan," said Peter Dunstan as they got in the back of the car. "Am I driving you home?"

"Yes, please," Tristan said, grinning.

"Did you have dinner, Lexi?" Peter asked as he drove.

"Um, no. But we had a lot of junk, so I'm not really hungry."

Tristan stared at her and mouthed, "We just had sorbet."

Miming a slit throat, Alexandra mouthed back, "I'm not hungry, and they're annoying." Tristan nodded. They spent the rest of the car ride imitating Sequoia for both Peter's and their own amusement.

As they got out of the car, Peter said, "Are you okay, Lexi? You don't look so well."

"I'm *fine*, Dad," Alexandra replied angrily. "I'm just tired. I couldn't sleep last night."

As she walked up the steps and into the house, Alexandra felt like crying. Emma ran up to her excitedly.

"Lexi, guess what? My teacher is taking us all to the pool on Friday, because we were really well behaved this week!"

"Cool," said Alexandra impatiently.

"She already ate downtown, with her friend Tristan," Peter called to Beth.

"Who?"

"Tristan," Peter said in his normal voice, as Beth walked out of the kitchen. "You know, the tall, skinny one."

"They're all tall and skinny," Beth said, laughing. "Lexi, you look tired. Go to sleep early, okay?"

"Okay. I'm just going to do some homework and take a shower first."

Alexandra went upstairs, moving quickly. She closed the door to her room, threw her bag on the bed, took off her jacket, and fired it after the bag. She began digging through her drawers, and breathed a sigh of relief. The cookie and chocolate bar were both still there. Taking out a pair of pyjamas and a towel, she set them on the bed and unwrapped the chocolate bar, eating it as fast as she could. She wanted to cry. (*No, it's okay, it's okay,* she reminded herself.) Trying to slow down a bit, she also finished the cookie. When she went down the hall to the bathroom, the door was locked.. *Oh great,* she thought. *Emma's in the bathroom.* "Emma, get out of there quickly," she called through the door. "Please?"

"Okay, okay," Emma called back. "I'm just brushing my teeth."

As soon as Emma finished, Alexandra went into the bathroom and locked the door. She started the tap, tested the temperature, and then turned the shower on to muffle the noise. Then, she bent over the toilet and held her hair back to throw up.

In the shower, Alexandra felt her stomach happily. It was the same as before the chocolate and the cookie. She also didn't feel as panicky or depressed. Feeling along her jaw, she sighed. She had to stop doing this, and just not eat. It was making her face fat. She walked into her room, trying to hold onto the happiness until she could fall asleep, but it didn't work. Lying under the covers, Alexandra tried to block everything out of her head, but she couldn't, and she started crying into her pillow. "I hate you, I hate you!" she mouthed angrily into the darkness, not sure who she meant. Eventually, calmed and exhausted from crying, Alexandra fell asleep.

Chapter Four

Julian Reese
They don't teach us the ABC's, We play on the hard concrete, All we've got is life on the streets, All we've got is life on the streets ... I want an accent, something non-Canadian.

Julian woke up to his alarm clock for the first time since he had arrived in Vancouver. He got up, glad not to be waking up an hour before the alarm. It was so quiet in his homestay that early. Everyone else got up at around the same time. It wasn't like his home, where if he got up before anyone else he could just make his breakfast or whatever. Here, he was given breakfast at the time he was supposed to have breakfast, and he was pretty sure that he was not supposed to go wandering about the house when nobody else was up.

Standing up and stretching, he felt his hamstrings wince. He liked Mr. Yu, he was funny, but his classes were *hard*. He picked up his iPod from under his pillow, where he had put it the night before, and put in the earbuds. Sitting back down on the bed, he scrolled through his playlists. *There it is,* he thought, clicking on "wake." He mouthed the words to "Night Train" for the millionth time, laughing at his reflection in the mirror. *Axl Rose I am not,* he thought as he picked out his clothes.

As he ate his cereal, he listened to Keiko argue with Mr. Yu. "If you want skim milk, I'm not going to waste my money," said Mr. Yu. "You want skim milk, take this milk, put water in. There, skim milk."

Julian wished that there was someone in his home-stay who went to school with him. But they had all graduated (or, in Keiko's case, had opted out of senior school, only graduating from middle school in Japan), and were in the youth company at the academy. As he waited for the bus, Julian shivered. Going to school at 6:30 in the morning sucked, but it was the only way to get enough credits to graduate while going to the academy every day. *You* could *have done a distance course,* he told himself reproachfully. *But no way would that would have gotten done.* He began kicking a rock from one foot to the other, distracting himself from the cold and his boredom. "Aaand Beckham goes for the net," he said under his breath, attempting to hit the bus-stop pole. He missed and the rock shot into the street, where it was run over. Julian looked at it sadly. "Sorry, old fellow," he whispered, placing his hand on his heart. He looked up the street. The bus was coming.

As Tristan and Julian walked out of school, Julian couldn't stop laughing. "Did you see Ms. Mullen's face?"

"Yeah, but she still didn't give you any marks for it!" Tristan said, laughing at him.

"Oh, who cares!"

"Oh no, there's the bus! We've missed it ..."

"No, we haven't," Julian said, breaking into a run. "Come on, hurry!"

"We are so not going to make it." Tristan started running anyway. The bus driver waited for them patiently. They were out of breath as they got on the bus.

"Thanks," Julian said, smiling at the bus driver.

"Come on, we can sit here," Tristan called impatiently. "Oh, did you know we have rehearsal today?"

"What?" Julian was confused. He sat down beside Tristan, and Alexandra moved over to make room for him. "I thought we didn't have rehearsal until tomorrow? It's always on Saturday, isn't it?"

"No, we have rehearsal tonight, after class, for Rose and Sugarplum and Arabian leads, and Russian," Alexandra explained. "No Dmitri yet, though, because they'd have to pay him. It's leads and corps together that are rehearsing tomorrow."

"Oh," said Julian. "Are we going to have time to go home and get dinner?"

"No, there's only an hour break," Tristan answered as he wrestled his lunch out of his backpack. "We can go get sushi, though. There's a really good place right next to the academy."

"Cool."

"Do you want to come with us, Lexi?" Tristan asked casually.

"Um, I'll see okay?" Alexandra answered. "I think I might be going to get dinner with Grace. But I really want sushi, so maybe I'll come with you anyway." She shot a glance to the front of the bus, where Anna and

Grace were sitting together. She took her juice box out and jabbed the straw in violently.

"Okay, cool," Tristan said, making an effort not to look at her.

"Hey, are you guys going to get sushi later?" asked Taylor from the seat in the corner. Julian looked up, surprised.

"Yeah, wanna come?" he asked. Tristan kicked him.

"Where's Kaitlyn?" Tristan asked Taylor pointedly.

"Oh, she's sick," said Taylor happily. "She phoned me last night and asked me to tell everyone that she can't come in today because she's, like, sick. I would really like to come. I love sushi." She smiled brightly at Julian. Tristan groaned and sank into his seat, sprawling his legs into the aisle. Alexandra ignored them and concentrated on her juice box.

As they went into the changing room, Tristan punched Julian on the shoulder. "Ow, what was that for?"

"Getting in touch with my 'masculine side.' Why did you have to invite Taylor?" He rummaged through his locker for a clean shirt, picked one up, and smelled it. "Ugh!" he threw it back in and tried another. "I mean, she's so annoying. It would have been cool with just the three of us."

"Oh," said Julian. "Sorry. I didn't know you didn't like her. She just seemed like she really wanted to come."

"Yes, that doesn't mean you have to invite her!" said Tristan patiently. "And I didn't say I disliked her. I just said that she was annoying."

Kageki leisurely wandered into the changing room.

"Where were you?" Tristan asked.

"I missed the bus?"

"Do you—" started Julian.

"Jules, do you have an extra shirt?" Tristan asked quickly, cutting Julian off. Julian gave him an annoyed look.

"No!"

"That's okay." Tristan smiled sweetly.

Walking up the stairs, Julian whispered angrily to Tristan, "I thought you and Kageki were tight!"

"We are! That doesn't mean that the whole school has to come with us. Try to hurry after class, okay? Maybe we can 'accidentally' forget that Taylor wanted to come." Julian sighed.

Upstairs, all the girls were putting on their *pointe* shoes. "We have Mr. Moretti today, apparently," Tristan said. "I am too tired for his class today."

"I don't like his class," Julian said, putting his soft shoes on the wrong feet and trying again.

"You just don't like him because of how he says your name," Tristan laughed. "*Juuuuliiiiiaaaan.*"

"No, I just don't like his class." Julian was defensive. He was still annoyed at Tristan. He rolled into the middle splits and put his earbuds in.

Mr. Moretti came into the class without anyone realizing. He stood there for a few minutes, waiting to see if anyone would notice. As they continued to talk and stretch, he frowned and walked to the centre. "Children," he said quietly. "Is this a coffee shop? Would you like some tea perhaps? Coffee? Possibly a cookie?"

They quickly unplugged and started shedding layers of clothing. "Had a good lunch, *baby*?" he asked Angela, smiling sweetly at her. "It looks it." He walked to the *barre* and began leading class. "One, two, *in*, point your footsies, babies!"

After class, Julian turned to Tristan. "Is it just me, or does Mr. Moretti totally creep you out?"

"Oh, it's just Mr. Moretti," Tristan shrugged. "I think he secretly wishes he could work for the CIA or be a pilot or something." He saw Taylor and mouthed, "Hurry up."

"No," Julian mouthed back firmly. But they ran down the stairs to get changed.

"Hey, Lexi," Tristan said hopefully from the door of the boy's changing room as Alexandra walked downstairs. "You coming for sushi?"

"Oh, yeah," she said, surprised. "I said I was going to, didn't I?"

"Um, yeah, right," said Tristan. "Me and Jules will be out in a sec."

As they left the academy, Taylor kept up a running commentary. "I really liked class today, didn't you? I just love Mr. Moretti's classes. Oh, are we not going in there? You're right. The other place has much better sushi doesn't it? Omigod, I am such a dumb blond. I totally forgot to bring my school stuff out of my locker. It's okay, though, I never do my homework anyway." The other three kept silent, with their own thoughts to occupy them. Taylor eventually ran out of steam and walked silently, watching them nervously.

"Is Russian hard?" Julian asked suddenly, turning to Tristan.

"Oh, no. I mean, it's really tiring, but you'll be fine."

Relieved, Julian quickened his pace. Tristan and Alexandra drew abreast of him and matched it. Taylor was forced to walk behind them as there was no more room beside them.

"Mr. Moretti is really hard in rehearsal, though," Alexandra said. "I mean, that's good, but if you're not used to it, it can be pretty tough. Like, he gets really mad if you don't remember every correction and apply it the second he says it."

"Yeah. And once he threw the CD player at somebody who kept messing up," Tristan snickered. "And then he kicked them out of the show." Taylor fell back a little more — that was her.

"But you're a boy, so they won't kick *you* out," Alexandra reassured him, patting his shoulder. "They totally need you."

They'd arrived at the sushi restaurant.

"Do we have time to eat there?" Alexandra asked.

Tristan checked his cell. "Yup. Come on. This place is awesome."

As they went in, Julian stopped suddenly. "This is the same song Keiko was playing last night!"

Tristan rolled his eyes. "Keiko is Japanese," he said as if explaining something to a three-year-old. "So is this restaurant. So they have the same music."

"Hey, it's still cool," Julian blushed. "They don't really have very good Japanese restaurants on the

Island or in Toronto."

Once they sat down, Alexandra kept tapping her nails on the table.

"'Sup?" asked Tristan.

"I'm really nervous for rehearsal tonight," she admitted. "Mr. Moretti totally hates me."

Tristan didn't disagree.

"Hey, but you're really good!" Julian said, confused. "I saw you on YouTube ... I mean, I looked because you got bronze, right? So I thought you might have something up. And you were awesome, and you are in class, too. Why do you think he doesn't like you?"

"He just doesn't." Alexandra kicked the table leg lightly and repeatedly while trying not to cry. Tristan nodded. The waiter came over, and they began to order, relieved for the interruption. Tristan and Alexandra decided to split a sushi combo and ordered a boat combo with tempura for Julian.

"So you can decide what you like," said Alexandra.

"And because we want to steal the apple slices that come with it," added Tristan.

"And what do you want, dear?" asked the waitress, smiling at Taylor.

"Um, can I have the same as him?" She pointed at Julian. "I like tempura," she added with an apologetic giggle as Tristan and Alexandra looked at her in disgust. "I don't like the apple slices, though, you guys can have them if you want."

"As if you're going to be able to finish that," said Alexandra.

"I like the boat, it's pretty," Taylor said more confidently.

"Whatever," Alexandra said, exchanging a *Do you believe her?* look with Tristan. Meanwhile, the waitress had come over with tea, and Julian was smelling it excitedly.

"This is so cool!" he said. "It smells like rice."

"Have you not even ever had green tea before?" Alexandra asked in disbelief.

"Not *this* kind!"

"You are so weird," laughed Tristan.

"Yeah, you totally fit in here," Alexandra said, laughing. Taylor went to the washroom while they waited for the sushi.

"Hey, pass that," Tristan said to Alexandra, pointing at Taylor's glass of water. Alexandra laughed and passed it.

"What are you doing?" Julian asked.

"Wait and see," Tristan said gleefully, opening a packet of salt and pouring it in the glass.

"You can do at least three more before you can see the salt," Alexandra said, watching the salt sink into the water.

"Guys, seriously," Julian protested. "Isn't that a little mean? And elementary school?"

"Nope," Tristan said, quickly sliding the glass back into its place and stuffing the salt wrappers in his bag.

"Besides, she's annoying," Alexandra added. Taylor came back with a big smile.

"Guess what?" she said. "The waitress lady gave me a free Coke! Isn't that cool? She said I looked cute!"

Julian kicked Tristan. "Karma," he whispered.

The waitress came over with the food, and Julian took his boat in surprise. "When they say boat, they really mean it, eh?" Tristan and Alexandra laughed. Taylor smiled at him while rearranging her food on the table.

"I know, right?" she said. "When I first had this, I was like 'What the F?' Actually I wasn't, because I was like three, but I would've. I was really upset, though, because they don't let you take them home."

"I should think not," Julian said, looking his over with amazement. "It's all wood, and the carvings are really cool. I am so showing my family this place when they come to get me at Christmas."

When they left the restaurant, Taylor went home because she didn't have rehearsal.

"Bye," Julian said absently as they left.

"Bye," she said, her face dropping as Tristan and Alexandra ignored her.

As they walked down the street, they heard some- one call "Hey! Faaattiiiiies!"

They turned around. "Oh, it's Grace … and Aiko and Anna," said Alexandra. "Fatties yourselves!" she called back across the street. Laughing, both groups headed back to the academy.

As the girls put on their *pointe* shoes, Aiko asked, "Where's Kaitlyn? I thought she was also Rose, with Anna?"

"I don't know," said Anna. "Mr. Moretti is going be furious." She grinned in anticipation.

"Where are Jonathon and Leon?" Alexandra asked.

"They're downstairs with Tristan and Kageki," Julian said. They heard yells coming from downstairs.

"I wonder who they locked out this time," Grace sighed.

"Sounds like Jonathon," Julian said, listening intently. "And I think he's naked."

"Eww, gross! Jonathon naked?" Alexandra grimaced. "So not wanting that picture in my mind."

"Would you rather Dmitri?" Anna asked, laughing.

"No!" Alexandra said, disgusted. "They are both completely repulsive. I wish they would either improve a hundred percent and get a job away from here, or just look in the mirror and give up."

"Harsh, but true," Grace said. "Just wait, in a few minutes you'll get to do *pas*, with Jonathon and Leon!"

"Omigod, I can't wait," Alexandra said sarcastically.

The door opened, and Mr. Moretti said, "Come in, babies. Where are the other gentlemen?" he asked Julian, frowning.

"Uh …" Julian started, but at that moment there was a thundering up the stairs and the boys ran in giggling.

"Uh, sorry, sir," Tristan said, holding his hands behind his back, rocking on his heels. "We didn't know you were starting early." He looked up at the clock, trying to keep from smirking. The clock read 6:28.

"Very humorous, Tristan," Mr. Moretti said, his mouth slowly stretching into a Cheshire cat smile, which then disappeared. "Come in, everyone. I think we will perhaps start with the Rose," he said meditatively. "Anna first.…Where is Kaitlyn?" he asked, frowning as he noticed she was missing.

"We don't know." Anna was clearly enjoying herself.

"Well, does she know that this is a rehearsal for her?"

"Yes," Anna said.

"I will not have people missing my rehearsals," Mr. Moretti said with cold fury. "If Kaitlyn thinks that she can just miss rehearsals, she is very mistaken. If she manages to show up tomorrow, please inform her that she is no longer being considered for this role. Anna, you will do the full role."

Nobody dared mention that Anna was also half Arabian, but, scanning the students, Mr. Moretti realized this by himself. "Yes …," he said thoughtfully. "Anna, you will prepare to do both casts of Rose, as well as Arabian. We will finalize later. No one is guaranteed a role just because they have been cast. It will change if things do not work, if *you* do not work. Anna, we will still start rehearsing with you. The rest of you, go warm yourselves on the side, and girls learn Anna's part. Everyone should be able to do every part. Believe me, I will check. Aiko, if you still remember from last year, you may teach Grace."

He started to walk over to the CD player, but abruptly turned around, seeing Alexandra yawn in the mirror. "Alexandra. Are we boring you…?"

"Uh, n-no," Alexandra stuttered, quickly dropping her hand from her mouth, hiding it behind her back.

"Do let us know if we are boring you, Alexandra. Or if you are perhaps tired, feel free to go home, baby. Don't let *us* keep you."

Alexandra ducked her head and wiggled her feet around uncomfortably, muttering, "Sorry."

"Do you see Anna sleeping?" Mr. Moretti continued. "You are the kind of student I hate to teach, the ones that make me want to quit. One student that just doesn't bother, is too lazy to make an effort, these students bring down the entire class. You watch the class, and it would be good, clean work, except one student is always wrong, and that student is you. You never improve, you never listen. You think that you always know better than me, don't you? You know what, if you don't want to be here, just get out. I said, get out!"

Alexandra stood in place, not moving, keeping her face blank.

"Did you hear me?" Mr. Moretti screamed, coming to stand right in front of Alexandra, almost touching her. She stood perfectly still, staring straight ahead. For some reason the *Winnie the Pooh* theme song popped into her head, and she focused her brain on remembering all the words to it. "Fine, stay," Mr. Moretti said, his voice soft and oh-so-quiet. "You always do what you want to anyway, why should this time be any different? You have no respect for anyone but yourself."

Giving a little laugh, he walked back to Anna.

"Now Anna, sweetie, I want you to really focus on your *port de bras* for this solo," Mr. Moretti said, the Cheshire cat smile on his face once again. Alexandra stood still for a second, quickly blocking what just happened. *Just concentrate on your work, don't think about it right now, and pretend it didn't happen,* she told herself, making her body relax. *Breathe, don't cry,* she told herself as she walked over to the side and began learning the Rose solo.

"Wow," Julian whispered. "She was right. He really doesn't like her."

"Nope, he doesn't," Tristan whispered back. "That wasn't actually so bad. Last year, he told her that she made him sick and if she didn't get out of his sight he'd throw up."

As Mr. Moretti worked with Anna, Aiko and Grace worked together. Alexandra tried to look interested in Mr. Moretti's corrections for Anna and learn the Rose solo. Leon, Jonathon, and Kageki sat just outside of the studio playing on their Nintendo DSs. Julian and Tristan were bored. After they had stretched for as long as they thought they could, they went and sat on the piano bench, slouching so the piano hid them and they could talk.

"Do you think this would be safe to drink?" Julian asked, picking up a half empty lychee juice box from on top of the piano's key cover.

"Gross, no! That's been there for three days. George just keeps moving it onto the floor in the morning and putting it back when he goes home."

"Why?"

"Um, I think to see if some idiot like you would drink it!" Tristan raised his eyebrows.

"Right, makes sense." Julian gingerly placed the juice box back.

"Do you think he's actually going to rehearse any-one but Anna tonight?" Tristan sighed. "Or is he just going to make us sit here for fun, like he usually does, or because the Demidovskis said he had to rehearse us?"

"Well, I'd read the clock and see if he has any time to rehearse us, but I am way too lazy to read an analog clock right now."

"Don't worry! Tristan to the rescue." said Tristan sleepily, digging his cell out of his warm-ups. "It's 7:58, so we have two minutes to rehearse. And it is completely pathetic that we are so tired right now!"

"Poor Alexandra and Anna," Julian said, smothering a yawn.

"Better them than us, Jules. Wait 'til you've been introduced to the Russian choreography."

"Okay, finished," Mr. Moretti said. The boys rushed downstairs, eager to go home. The girls limped to the hallway to take off their shoes before they attempted the stairs.

As they got changed Julian said, "Did you notice that he didn't even apologize or anything?"

Tristan laughed. "If he had, he'd have to be sorry. And he's not."

"Right," sighed Julian. "He's a total creeper."

Tristan laughed. "You think that's creepy? You should see his wife."

"His wife's creepy, too? That's funny."

"No, no," Tristan laughed. "I mean, his wife used to be a student at the academy. There's like a twenty- or twenty-five-year age gap between them. They got married after she graduated. She was a Korean student and hardly spoke any English at all, and he sure as hell doesn't speak any Korean."

"Wow!" Julian whistled.

"Yeah! Come on, let's go,"

As they walked to the bus, Julian asked, "So what is going to happen to Kaitlyn? Did he actually mean it when he kicked her out?"

"Yes, of course he meant it. But Anna can't do both roles at once, and Mr. Moretti certainly won't give Alexandra both casts of Arabian." He swung his back pack to the ground and rummaged through it for his bus pass. "Mr. Demidovski will probably do something about it tomorrow. Besides, they need understudies." They got on the bus and sat across from a highly high individual by accident.

"Do you know whatsa good about coke?" he asked them.

"*Look out the window,*" Tristan whispered to Julian.

"It makes you freakin' better, everything better. Hell, this whole freakin' city shoulda take coke." The druggie started rubbing snot from his nose to his cheek. As the bus lurched, the druggie lurched and fell into the bus aisle. Not at all fazed, he got up again, hauling on the bus bars. He noticed his bag of garbage, which he had left on the seat during his fall. "Bag a freakin' crap, bag a freakin' crap-garbage," he said angrily. Falling against the bench, again, he reached up and tried to push open the window.

"Should we move to the front?" Julian whispered while the druggie was trying to open the window.

"Nah, he'll just get pissed at us," said Tristan. When he had managed to pry open the window, the druggie started to push the garbage through the window. As they were at a stop sign, the garbage fell directly on the neighbouring car's hood. The druggie began to laugh gleefully.

"Bag o'crap man, bag o' freakin' crap," he chortled happily. "Waddyou think 'bout that, huh? Freakin' hell, man." As teetered toward their bench, Julian and Tristan moved to the front and started giggling

"Shit, that was funny," whispered Julian.

"Bag o'freakin' crap man," replied Tristan. "Get it right! Oh hell, man!" They both collapsed into laughter again.

Julian got into bed and turned out his light. *Oh great,* he thought. *I forgot to call Will and Daisy again.* And now he was too tired. Sighing, he turned on his lamp and managed to reach his laptop off his desk without getting out of bed. Pleased with himself, he flipped it open. He logged onto Facebook and sent Will a message:

> Having fun, sorry forgot to phone you again.
> Will phone you tomorrow. It's really funny here.
>
> Love,
> Jules

He smiled at his dad's profile pic. Will had put a picture of himself holding River, who was modelling one of Daisy's tie-dye shirts.

He put his laptop on the floor, too lazy to put it back on his desk, and turned on his iPod. *Only a few minutes,* he told himself as he listened, slowly falling asleep.

Chapter Five

Kaitlyn Wardle
I am Rose and Clara for VIBA's Nutcracker!! :)

Kaitlyn walked into the academy, waving to Gabriel on the way in.

Gabriel looked at her nervously. "Um, hello," he said, quickly ducking his head and focusing on his paper-work. Kaitlyn shook her head as she walked over to the schedule. *The staff here just keeps getting weirder.* She sneezed, not quite over her cold yet. She scanned the schedule and casting lists, skipping over the corps bits to concentrate on the principal parts as she searched for her name.

First act rehearsal for Clara, then an hour break while Russian rehearsed, then Rose ... Kaitlyn looked at the casting list again, and laughed. *The office-staff are such idiots,* she thought. *They only put Anna's name under Rose. How does that even make sense? How can Anna do both casts of Rose?* Mr. Demidovski came out of the office and started slightly when he saw her.

"And how are *you*?" he asked, bowing slightly and putting his hand on her shoulder.

"Great, thank you, Mr. Demidovski."

"Yes, yes, that is good...." Mr. Demidovski looked a bit pained. "Working hard, eh? Good girl." He released her shoulder and smiled. Kaitlyn walked down the hall, rolling her eyes as she saw Tristan.

"Did you see that?" she asked. "Mr. Demidovski is so weird." Tristan ignored her, and continued listening to Anna and Jessica. Kaitlyn stood there, puzzled, before going downstairs, slightly disturbed.

"Hey, Kaitlyn," Taylor said as Kaitlyn came into the bathroom. She calmly continued to do her bun, not even turning around to look at Kaitlyn.

"It's good to be back and not sick anymore," Kaitlyn tried.

"Oh, right, you were sick. Don't forget my party is tonight." She frowned at her bangs and attacked them with so much hairspray, she could probably cause global warming single-handedly.

"Oh, yeah, when is it again?" Kaitlyn tried to act casual and pretend she had forgotten.

"You are *so stupid*, Kaitlyn," Taylor giggled so Kaitlyn couldn't take offense. "It's at seven-ish. A bunch of us are going to Delilah's house after rehearsal to get ready and then we're meeting the boys and Anna, Aiko, Grace, and Alexandra at the academy at 6:30 and bussing, so you could meet us then if you want." Kaitlyn stared at her. Taylor pretended she didn't notice, selecting a sparkly pin to stick in her bun.

"Does my bun look flat?" Taylor asked as she stuck the pin in.

"Yes, It looks fine." Kaitlyn slammed her bag down

on the counter and took out her clean dance clothes.

"Oh … you're wearing that?" Taylor eyed Kaitlyn's bodysuit in surprise.

"Yeah. What's wrong with it?"

"It's just … really white. I didn't know you liked white."

"What do you mean? Everyone likes white, why would I hate white? I never said I didn't like white."

Keiko had come in, and when she saw the bodysuit Kaitlyn was holding, she looked Kaitlyn up and down, horrified. "You're wearing that?"

"Why does nobody like white around here?" asked Kaitlyn.

"Because it makes you look like a beached whale," Keiko said. "Taylor, you can totally wear it, though."

"I'm just so tiny!" Taylor was glad for the recognition.

"Well, it's the only bodysuit I brought, okay?" Kaitlyn said defensively. She went unhappily to the stalls to get changed. When she went upstairs, she self-consciously sucked in her stomach as much as she could and hoped that her thick-looking thighs would be attributed to her warm-ups. She sat down in the hallway to stretch, alone. Everyone was in their own groups, and nobody invited her to sit with them. She wondered why and sighed. *It can't be intentional,* she told herself. She stuck her foot out, admiring the arch. She looked around to see if anybody else had noticed.

Instead she heard Tristan, who was stretching Anna's feet, say, "Anna, your feet make me sick! Can I, like, chop them off you, so I can have them?" Anna giggled happily. Kaitlyn listened in disbelief. *Anna's feet can't even remotely compare to mine!* she thought angrily.

Finally, Taylor and Keiko came upstairs, and Kaitlyn smiled, relieved. But they passed by without even looking at her. They went to sit with a group of the Japanese students against the wall by the door to the studio. Kaitlyn watched them giggle as they huddled about some manga book.

Taylor was in hysterics. "Pornographic comics?" she rolled on the floor, laughing hard. "Doesn't that defeat the point?"

"Look, look!" Keiko said excitedly. "Now on subway!" They all leaned forward to get a closer look.

Feeling self-conscious, Kaitlyn went over and sat next to them. "Whose are those?" she asked uncomfortably.

"Kageki's," Keiko said without turning round. "I stole them out of his locker this morning. He still hasn't noticed that they're gone." Just at that moment, Kageki came thundering up the stairs, and Keiko quickly stuffed the books under her bag.

"Where are they?" said Kageki, looking at Keiko and the other girls. Mao giggled.

"What?" Keiko looked up at him innocently. They all began arguing in Japanese. Keiko quietly translated it to Taylor. Kaitlyn scooted away, feeling even more awkward, and began putting on her *pointe* shoes.

Chloe came up to her, smiling sweetly. "I'm so glad we are Clara together! I can't wait to start rehearsing, can you?"

Michael came up and sat down next to them. "Chloe is really pleased that she got the part," he informed Kaitlyn. "I'm quite pleased with my own role of Fritz as well. I am glad the Demidovskis recognized that I am capable of it."

Kaitlyn looked around to see if anyone had noticed that she was sitting with the two little kids, but nobody was paying any attention. "Yeah, I like doing Clara. I've done the role several times before, actually. I am excited to do Rose though, that's one role I haven't done before. I was Sugarplum fairy last year."

"I didn't know you were doing Rose," Michael said with fake enthusiasm. "I didn't see it on the board."

"Oh, that's just the office staff's fault." Kaitlyn tried to sound unconcerned. "I am doing Rose one cast, and Clara one cast."

"Oh. Well, I am sure you will be a great Rose.... And Clara. Both of you."

Chloe smiled at him. "You're so nice, Michael!"

"Thank you, Chloe," Michael said, widening his eyes. Kaitlyn gazed intently at his eyelashes, wondering if they were dyed.

Mr. Moretti opened the studio door and called them in. As Kaitlyn passed by, Mr. Moretti frowned. "Ah, Kaitlyn," he said softly, but everyone went silent so they could listen. "I am so glad that you were able to join us."

Kaitlyn frowned, confused. "Why wouldn't I be able to come?"

"I don't know. Why don't you tell me?"

"Oh!" she said, suddenly realizing what he meant. "You mean because I wasn't here on Friday?"

"Yes, finally the light comes." Mr. Moretti was sarcastic.

"Oh, I was sick on Friday. I told Taylor to tell you."

"Oh, and you did not think to inform me yourself?" Mr. Moretti was smiling his Cheshire cat smile. "You thought it would be better to make Taylor do this? Might I suggest choosing someone with a brain next time?" The students giggled behind him.

Taylor blushed and smiled. "It's not my fault I'm not smart."

"Missing rehearsal is not acceptable," Mr. Moretti said. "As this is the first time, you have only lost the role of Rose. Do it again, and you will be out of the show. If you are really ill, you come here and watch or mark. I do not have the patience to teach things repeatedly just because someone is lazy and does not care."

Kaitlyn mouth fell open in shock. The scene over, everyone began talking again, shedding their warm-ups and stretching their feet. Nobody looked at Kaitlyn. It was as if she didn't exist. Mr. Moretti began setting the prologue.

As Taylor walked by, Kaitlyn grabbed her arm. "Why didn't you tell him that I was sick?"

"I forgot! Besides, you should have phoned in yourself."

"Well, you didn't tell me that, did you?"

"I forgot," Taylor wrestled her arm out of Kaitlyn's grasp. Kaitlyn stood there, trying not to cry. *What is Mom going to say?* she thought, careful not to make eye contact with anyone. *How can I tell everyone that I'm not Rose?* she thought, suddenly panicking as she remembered she'd already told everyone that she was. Mr. Moretti called her over as if nothing was wrong.

"Ah, Kaitlyn, Chloe. The Clara is sitting here with her Mama, admiring her. Come on, Kaitlyn, do it first. Sit on the stool while your Mama fixes your curls. No, that is all wrong. Act happy, you think you look beautiful. Chloe, you try. Yes, that is right. Kaitlyn, study the way Chloe does this, you need to learn from her." Kaitlyn glared at Chloe, who ignored her and smiled up at Mr. Moretti.

"Now, it is dancing with the dolls."

Finally, Kaitlyn thought. Mr. Moretti had been working on the parents' dance for the last hour.

"Chloe first," Mr. Moretti said. Kaitlyn clenched her hands into fists at her side. The first cast was supposed to get to try first. *If he doesn't stop trying to infuriate me, I am going to kill that man. Or my mother will.* She felt a bit happier at the image of Mr. Moretti dead. *Of course!* Kaitlyn thought suddenly, relieved. *The Demidovskis won't let him do this. Mom said they promised me Rose and Clara!* She smiled, problem solved.

"Kaitlyn! Are we *boring* you?" asked Mr. Moretti. "Could you *attempt* to pay attention? I am not going to repeat this, so you had better concentrate. If you don't know what to do, Chloe does." Kaitlyn glared at him and wondered if the Demidovskis would fire him for not obeying their orders about casting.

After rehearsal, Kaitlyn was still angry. Even if he couldn't really take Rose away from her, it was still humiliating. And now she'd had two less rehearsals of the role than Anna. She slammed her locker door shut and went upstairs, not saying goodbye to anyone. She didn't notice that no one said goodbye to her either, not even Taylor.

As she got in the car, she felt relieved. Her mom would fix this. "Mom, you would not believe what happened today!"

"What?" Cecilia pulled out of the parking space.

"Mr. Moretti kicked me out of Rose! He said it was because I missed a rehearsal, when I was sick. And he said that it wasn't okay to miss rehearsals, even if you are sick, and that I should have told him personally. He was really mad about that, because Taylor never told him that I was sick, because she 'forgot,' and he said that I shouldn't have told her because she didn't have a brain."

"That is not okay! Taylor should be in trouble for not telling him, not you. And what on earth is that about you having to come in even if you are sick?"

"He said you have to come in and sit or mark on the side, even if you're sick!" Kaitlyn relaxed into her seat, relieved that her mom could take care of it now.

"Well, that is just ridiculous. What, does he want the rest of the school to get sick as well? Don't worry, I will go in and talk to Mr. and Mrs. Demidovski tomorrow. We'll get this all sorted out. I can't believe he did that!"

"Thanks, Mom." Kaitlyn felt slightly bored of the whole thing now that her mom was taking care of it. "And he kept having Chloe rehearse Clara before me."

"Well, we'll discuss that too," Cecilia said firmly. "Are you excited about Taylor's party tonight?"

"Oh … yeah. But everyone was being really weird today. Even Taylor."

"Don't worry about that, Kaitlyn. They will be fine after I talk to the Demidovskis. Just act confident and happy at the party. Where is it, anyway?"

"Um, I don't really know," Kaitlyn sighed. "I'm supposed to meet everyone at the academy at 6:30 and then we're bussing. Because everyone's going to Delilah's to get ready, except the people who have rehearsal."

"You didn't want to go?"

"I wasn't invited." Kaitlyn's voice broke.

"Oh, sweetie! It's okay. It'll all be fine after I talk to the Demidovskis. Were they weird before or after you found out that you weren't Rose?"

"Before."

"That sounds like they all knew before you did."

Kaitlyn started undoing her hair, scowling. "Pigs!"

Kaitlyn got ready for the party a little more happily. Her new dress was very pretty. It was green stretch velvet on the top with an empire waist, and a lighter green skirt. She brushed out her hair and put the dress on, admiring it in the mirror. Luckily it went just over the tops of her knees, so it wouldn't be too cold on the bus. She dug her black ballet flats out of the closet. Looking in the mirror, she considered lip gloss. She decided it was too much. It was just a birthday party,

"Ready?" Cecilia asked. "You look very pretty, dear."

Jeff came to look. "Yes, you do. Don't you have any shoes with a bit of a heel or something, though?"

"She's a dancer, Jeff." Cecelia said crossly. "Dancers don't wear heels. It ruins their feet."

"Oh. Okay, then. Have fun, phone us when it's about time for us to pick you up, and when you get to the restaurant so we know where you are."

"Okay, okay," Kaitlyn said. She had butterflies in her stomach, but it was a good kind of nervous. *It's just a birthday party, geez,* she told herself.

"Do you have Taylor's present?" Cecilia asked as she started the car.

Kaitlyn dug in her bag to double check. Yes, it was still there. She'd bought Taylor a sparkly pin from Charmed Designs. As they pulled up to the academy, Cecilia reminded her to phone.

"Mom, I won't forget," Kaitlyn groaned. "Bye, love you." She got out of the car and walked into the academy. She could hear everyone downstairs talking, so she went to join them. *Omigod,* she thought, *Everyone looks like they're going to the Oscars or something.*

"Hey Kaitlyn," Taylor said. She was in the middle of curling her hair. "Why aren't you ready yet?"

"I am."

"Oh. Are you going to wear those shoes?"

Kaitlyn realized that all the girls were wearing extraordinarily high, sparkly, colourful heels. She'd always wondered who bought those shoes.

"Yes. Dancers shouldn't wear heels, they are bad for

your feet." Keiko and Taylor laughed.

"Yeah, right," Delilah snorted, adjusting her purple bra. Tristan came running into the girl's bathroom.

"Does this look all right?" he asked Alexandra and Anna, twirling. "Gel or no gel?"

"Definitely gel," said Alexandra, carefully applying more eyeliner. "Sparkles or no?" she asked, pointing at her eyes. Tristan swung himself on top of the counter and peered at her eyes.

"What colour?"

"Silver eyeliner sparkles."

"Wow, for sure! Can I use some of your gel?" he asked Grace.

Grace was straightening her hair and passed Tristan the gel. He began carefully combing it in, forming soft waves and peaks, framing his face perfectly. Kaitlyn looked around at the dresses. They were all colours and styles, and they were all "down to there and up to here," as her mom would say. She looked down at her chest; it was definitely *not* "down to there." For the first time, she wished it was. Everyone at the academy was already fairly tall, and the heels just made it worse.

"Where are we going, Taylor?" Kaitlyn asked, standing awkwardly, trying to not look in the mirror.

"Oh, Earls on Robson." Taylor carefully applied red lipstick. "I tried to book Shabusen, but it was already full."

"Okay, sounds good," Kaitlyn was relieved. Apparently they just liked dressing up like this. You didn't have to dress up for Earls, even the one on Robson. Still, she thought it was going to be an awkward night. She admired Anna's dress and earrings. *I have to get my ears pierced now. I'll ask Mom to take me tomorrow.*

As they got on the bus, everyone ignored the curious glances from the rest of the passengers. Except Kaitlyn. She sat down, feeling uncomfortable and blushing. She didn't ride the buses that often; usually her mom or dad drove her.

"I love your dress," a drag queen gushed to Alexandra.

"Aww, thanks so much!" Alexandra said, smiling at her.

"Does anyone here have ID?" Julian asked Tristan.

"Yes, Sophia, Ella, and Leon do" Tristan said. "They'll order stuff."

"Yay!" Taylor giggled.

Kaitlyn looked out the window, wishing ... she wasn't really sure what. She didn't want to *not* be here, but she didn't feel old enough for this party. She hadn't known that all the older students were going to be invited to Taylor's party too. She'd just assumed that it would be only their age group.

At the restaurant, Taylor happily sat at the head of their table. Kaitlyn got stuck between Leon and Jessica, across from Jonathon. She looked wistfully up the table, where Alexandra, Julian, Tristan, Kageki, Anna, and Grace were sitting with Taylor. Taylor wouldn't shut up, but everyone was being fairly polite because it was her birthday and they wanted to be invited next year.

"Hey, what's up?" Jonathon smiled at Kaitlyn.

"Nothing much," she answered gratefully. There was an awkward silence, and Kaitlyn suddenly remembered that she had to call her parents. She got up and excused herself to go to the bathroom — she didn't want people to hear her make the call.

"Oh, I'll come with you," Jessica said brightly.

"Oh, okay, great!" Now she'd have to phone in front of Jessica. Kaitlyn was self-conscious as she made the call.

When they got back to the table, Aiko was recording Tristan and Kageki. They'd managed to convince the waitress to give them crayons, and were melting them in one of the table candles.

"There … is so much blood," Tristan said, sticking a red crayon into the candle and letting it drip around the edges. "Are you *scared*?" he whispered dramatically, sticking his face directly into Aiko's camera. "What's the yellow for?" he asked in his normal voice, turning to Kageki. Kageki was sticking the yellow crayon in the candle.

"Sun."

"Kageki, this is a *horror* film! You can't have sun in a horror film."

"Maybe there's sun in Japanese horror films," Julian suggested.

"No! There is *no* sun in horror films. Period!" Tristan said.

"This movie has sun," Kageki said decisively.

"It's like Disney," sighed Tristan, shrugging his shoulders and grabbing the blue crayon. "This is bluebirds, 'kay?" He stuck the crayon into the candle.

Anna kicked him under the table. "The waitress is coming back!"

Tristan quickly blew out the candle and Kageki stuffed it under his napkin. Both of them turned and beamed at the waitress.

"Her boobs are really big," Grace whispered to Anna.

"Yeah, I think I'm going to be sick," Anna whispered back. "Do you think she realizes that the only reason she has such big boobs is because she's fat?"

"No. She looks pretty proud of them."

"I think Julian likes them," Grace giggled. Tristan overheard and glared at her.

As the waitress was about to leave with their orders, Tristan asked if they could have their picture taken with her.

"Alexandra, come on," Tristan said, grinning. Grace took the picture, trying not to laugh. As soon as the waitress left, everyone started passing Grace's camera around.

"Wow, her boobies are huge!" Taylor giggled. "I love how you two are sort of presenting them with your arms."

"This so better go on Facebook," laughed Delilah. Kaitlyn laughed with them, happy that she was a lot smaller than the waitress.

"Thank goodness," Delilah said dramatically as the food began to arrive. "I am starving."

They passed the food around and began trading. Aiko, Ella, Sophia, and Leon passed around four drinks and a tray of shooters.

"Can I take your salad? I'll give you my chicken and dinner roll," Alexandra asked Julian.

"Uh, sure." Julian was surprised.

"You can have half of my fries, too," Tristan offered.

"Hey, aren't you guys going to be hungry?" Julian asked, taking his second shot from Aiko.

"Nope," they both replied. Tristan moved Julian's salad to Alexandra's plate and dumped over half of his fries in the empty space.

"Anybody want my fries?" Jessica asked. There was a chorus of "nos," so Jessica picked up her water glass and dumped half of it on her fries.

"What did you do that for?" Kaitlyn asked in astonishment.

"It's this new trick I learned. Now that the fries are wet, I can't eat them."

Kaitlyn looked at the fries sadly.

"No, you sure can't. But it's such a waste of fries ..."

"What, would you rather that they went in someone's body, clogging up their arteries?" Jessica asked indignantly.

"No, I guess not." Kaitlyn began eating her wrap, but she wasn't as hungry as usual. Alexandra was dissecting her salad. She shoved Julian's salad to the side so that it didn't contaminate hers (it had salad dressing already mixed in). She began spearing bits of her salad and dipping it lightly into the small dish of dressing. Kaitlyn caught herself staring.

"Do you want some?" Jonathon asked Kaitlyn, pointing at the shot beside him.

"Um, no thank you."

Jonathon laughed. "Come on. Just try a sip. It tastes like juice."

Kaitlyn took a tiny sip. Surprised, she passed it back. "It *does* taste like juice."

"You didn't even have a teaspoon's worth. Wimp." Kaitlyn blushed. "Look at Julian!" Jonathon pointed up the table with his knife. "I think he's on his fifth already."

Kaitlyn looked up the table. Aiko was handing a very happy Julian a green shot, and Anna was explaining why hard alcohol was so much better than beer, because beer was really just empty calories. Taylor was telling everyone how much she liked lava lamps, because you could see the layers. Keiko said she wouldn't drink a lamp.

"You're drinking a bug!" Taylor exclaimed.

"A grasshopper's a bug?" Keiko asked, lifting up her drink and eying it suspiciously. Kaitlyn finished her dinner silently, then sat there drinking her sprite.

"Wow, you were hungry," Jessica said.

"What? Oh, no, not really," Kaitlyn said, waking up out of her reverie.

"Oh … it's just you finished your whole plate!"

Kaitlyn looked down at her plate and then around the table at the other half-full plates. She was embarrassed, so she crumpled up some napkins and put them on her plate, hoping that no one else would notice that she had finished her whole dinner. Tristan and Kageki were watching Julian drink shots. Many shots.

As they stood outside of Earls, everybody began dividing up according to their bus routes and car pools. Kaitlyn phoned her parents. Delilah's ears perked up.

"Are your parents picking you up?" she asked.

"Uh, yeah." Kaitlyn wondered if there was anything wrong with that.

"Oh, do you think I could get a ride then?" Delilah smiled at her for the first time. "I live really close."

"Oh, yeah, I'm sure you can." Kaitlyn was surprised and pleased. They spent several awkward and silent minutes waiting for Cecilia.

When they were in the car, Cecilia asked them about the party as they fastened their seat belts.

"Oh, it was great," Delilah said without waiting for Kaitlyn to speak. "Kaitlyn was way at the other end of the table, though, so I'm not really sure how it was down there, but whatevs!"

They drove home listening to a non-stop monologue from Delilah: what she thought about the academy, McKinley, Kaitlyn's dress, everyone else's dress, and the radio station Cecilia had chosen.

Chapter Six

Taylor Audley
Yay, Halloween!

Taylor walked to the bus slowly. She'd skipped math class. She hadn't wanted to, because now she had to explain it to her mom and get her to write a note, but if she had gone she'd have failed her test, for sure. And if she failed that test, she'd fail first term. *Maybe I can say I had a stomach-ache,* she thought. *No, then I'd have to miss Halloween tonight.* She sighed.

She turned to walk up to Kerrisdale Boulevard, not wanting to get to the academy too early. *I'll have to tell her that I would've failed,* she decided miserably. *Then she can decide what to do. It wasn't my fault, it was because rehearsals went on so long yesterday!* She debated where to go and decided on Starbucks. She shivered as she started walking; it was pouring rain, and it was all dripping down her back. She'd forgotten to bring an umbrella, as usual.

As she sat down with her pumpkin spice frappuccino, she sneezed violently. *Great, now I'm getting a cold.* When she finally got on the bus, she felt a bit more optimistic. The rain was getting warmer, and the clouds were starting to clear up.

Her cellphone started ringing as soon as she'd sat down. She checked her display; it was her mom. She groaned.

"Hi, Mom."

"Hello, Taylor. Where are you?"

"Um, on the bus to the academy? Where else would I be?" Taylor said, anxiously doing up her bag. She'd left it undone, and now all her papers were wet.

"I don't know, Taylor. Where would you be? I just got a call from your counsellor; he said that you didn't show up for math class today. He also said that you were supposed to have a test that determined whether or not you passed math this term." Her voice had gotten progressively shriller as she got more hysterical. Taylor quickly turned down the volume on her cell and debated hanging up. *No,* she decided. *Mom won't let me go out tonight if I hang up.*

"Mom, I wasn't going to pass the test."

"Taylor!" Charlize screeched. "I am not doing this! If you had shown up, you would have gotten some grade, and you might have had a prayer of passing math for the year. As it is …"

"I don't have a prayer?" Taylor asked innocently. Her mother became completely incomprehensible, so Taylor hung up. She dried off her earphones and turned on The Plain White T's. They were usually too calm for her, but today she needed calm. She bit her lip nervously as she thought about class today. It was Mrs. Castillo, and the last time Taylor had had class with her … well, it hadn't been fun. Mrs. Castillo had told the whole class that Taylor had the perfect body type for ballet, but no brain. The whole class had bullied her for weeks afterwards. It was going better so far this year though. When the graduating class left last year, so had many of the scariest people in the school. It had also helped that she had been cast so much better this year. Taylor took some red sprinkles out of her bag and absentmindedly shook some into her mouth.

Inside the academy, Taylor checked the schedule. It hadn't changed. They still had Mrs. Castillo. She went downstairs to get changed, dripping water all the way.

Taylor bent backwards over the *barre*, cracking her back. She heard everyone laughing and quickly swung up again. *Too fast!* She slumped against the *barre*, dizzy. When she could see again, she looked up. There was Leon in his Halloween costume. He was wearing small, black stretch shorts over top of fishnet tights, black ballet shoes, and a pink tank top. On top of this, he was wearing bunny ears, a large, red bunny nose, and was carrying a cat o'nine tails. Kageki ran over and got Anna to take a picture of him gazing adoringly into Leon's eyes with one leg wrapped around his hip, and then another of him kissing Leon's bunny nose.

Taylor got an idea. She quickly ran downstairs and rummaged through her bag. She pulled out her Barbie crown, and changed into her pink bodysuit and white wrap skirt. She eyed her reflection in the mirror approvingly, and ran upstairs. No one seemed to notice as she slowly opened the door. Everyone was too busy admiring Jonathon's costume to worry about hers. He was wearing uniform, but he had drawn obscene things all over his shirt, and was wearing sunglasses and earrings.

Mrs. Castillo came into the studio with a huge smile, her shawl floating behind her. Everyone snapped to attention. "Class! We start!" She frowned as she looked around the studio. "Ah, Halloween, yes? The trick or treat?" Everyone nodded. "Everyone to the *barre*. Okay." She began to lead the *barre* exercises, demonstrating each exercise dramatically.

As Mrs. Castillo was demonstrating the grand battements exercise, she caught Tristan looking at his butt in the mirror. "Tristan! Do not keep looking in the mirror! There are maybe one hundred perfect bodies in the world; you got one." Tristan turned away from the mirror, both pleased and embarrassed.

Taylor's crown started slipping when began doing the *pirouette* combination. Mrs. Castillo grabbed her arm and led her to the side. "Taylor! You wear too much jewellery. Crown today? Perhaps crown and necklace tomorrow? What the day after? Take off now!" Taylor quickly took off the crown, noticing that Mrs. Castillo hadn't made Leon take off his ears or nose.

After everyone had gone across the room, Mrs. Castillo worked on the boy's *grande allegro* while the girls were putting on their *pointe* shoes. Julian suddenly stopped, and asked to go get some ice. He'd turned on his ankle the wrong way.

Mrs. Castillo nodded absently, working on Tristan's *tour en l'aire*. "And push!" She was standing behind him, pushing his left shoulder as soon as he left the ground. "You must always land in fifth, not second!" Tristan came down off balance. Taylor tested her foot in her *pointe* shoes, wincing as soon as she put weight on it. Her Achilles was inflamed, again. She watched Mrs. Castillo nervously, trying to judge the right time to go ask if she could sit down.

"Are you going to sit out because of your ankle?" Keiko asked Taylor. Taylor nodded. "Okay, let's go ask together then. My knee's really hurting me."

"Mrs. Castillo, may I sit down because of my knee?" Keiko asked.

"Yes, yes, of course, Keiko. And what do you want?" Mrs. Castillo asked Taylor.

"Ah ... my ankle?" Taylor pointed at the ankle in question.

Mrs. Castillo sighed. "Again, this ankle? All right, sit down, but do some exercise by yourself. Do back, do stomach, work." She gestured Taylor to the side impatiently and turned back to the class. "*Adage*! One two, three four, breathe ... and draw up leg. Up, up, no up hip and unfold — no drop! Hold, and rise. *Coupé pas de bourée, pirouette en dedans* ... three at least please! You are the advanced students now, yes? *Coupé, ronds de jambe*, and *fondue* ... hold. Hold back attitude! Tristan, knee up! And *fondue* deeper, leg higher — yes!" Mrs. Castillo continued to call out exercises, then had the class mark it out to music.

At the end of class, Mrs. Castillo called the class over to her, having them make a semi-circle so she could give them a lecture. "Class, you must take care of your feet, your body. The choreographer is the artist, you are the brush, and your body, it is your paper. The feeling, the artistry is the paint, but you need the paper for the paint to be beautiful. Good, high-quality brush. And must be thin, strong paper. If you want to be the dancer, and have fat, you are fooling yourself. I don't care if you lie to your friends, your boyfriend, that is okay. But don't lie to yourself, don't cheat yourself, that is very stupid, eh? Do you understand me, Delilah? You know, if you don't drink water, lose maybe three pounds. Okay, finish!"

As everyone got changed, Taylor phoned her mom. "Mom, am I going home before I go out tonight? Or are we, like, going to dinner or something first? I need to know if I should get changed into my costume here."

Her mom sighed. "Taylor, I'm not even sure if I should let you go tonight. I can't believe you skipped that math test."

"Mom, I *have* to go. *Everyone's* going tonight."

"I know you *have* to go. I'm just not sure that I should be letting you. Taylor, you need to at least graduate from high school. Your counsellor has been unbelievably understanding by letting you stay in the super achievers program despite your grades, but you have to try. He wanted me to get you a tutor, but ..."

"Mom, I don't have time for a tutor."

"I know, that's what I told him. I'll let you go tonight, but you really have to try harder, okay? I've got to go."

Taylor hung up, trying not to cry. *And I still don't know whether I should get changed into my costume or not!* she thought. She sat there for a minute and listened to everyone talk about Halloween. She forced herself to stand and opened her locker, taking out a ROCKSTAR and a packet of sour gummy worms. Biting the top off of a worm, she sat back down, avoiding the pile of used toe tape beside her. *Gross!* She sneezed. The academy always had a weird smell from a mixture of tea tree oil, Tiger Balm, Chinese medicine, mould, and old costumes. Taylor had the feeling that she was allergic to it. She sneezed again and reached for a Kleenex.

"Bless you!" Keiko said. She sat down beside Taylor. "What are you dressing as tonight?"

"Same as for class. A Barbie princess. But I have a dress and stuff, too."

"I am dressing as butterfly."

"Cool!" said Taylor, gulping some of her ROCKSTAR.

"Quick, quick!" Kageki said, as he came thundering down the stairs. "Come upstairs! The third floor toilet is overflowing. It's coming through the ceiling!" Everybody ran upstairs.

The water was coming through the ceiling and pouring down the sliding door at the academy's side entrance, creating a waterfall. An enormous waterfall. "I didn't know the upstairs toilet *had* so much water!" Taylor shouted over the water.

"It was the one that just kept flushing. You know, the one that the little kids thought Moaning Myrtle lived in?" Kageki said. "So now they can't stop it from flooding!"

Outside, passersby stopped to look through the sliding doors, gazing at the waterfall in amazement. Julian grinned and waved at them.

Gabriel came bustling along, saying "Go, go! The plumber is coming, don't worry." He waved the people in the street away from the sliding door and shooed the students back downstairs.

"Alison, turn down that music!" Charlize said. She turned into Grandview Park. "Do you see your friends, Taylor?"

"No, but they're taking the bus. I'll call Keiko, though." Taylor hung up almost as soon as the phone connected. "Mom, they're right behind us!"

"Is Keiko the one in the butterfly costume?"

"Yes! Bye!" Taylor called over her shoulder as she ran out to meet them.

"Hey, Taylor!" said Keiko. "Are we going to go trick or treating first?"

"Nah, why don't we skip it?" Taylor said, seeing the expression on Delilah's face.

"Oh, yeah sure," Keiko said.

"Oh, look!" Delilah said excitedly as they heard music starting up. "The parade is starting." They pushed to the front of the crowd, murmuring apologies.

"There's the boys and the rest," Taylor said, looking across the street. Delilah waved at them, but they either didn't see her or didn't want to acknowledge that they had seen her. The drums started, and the crowd got quieter. People came running into the clear area and then stopped, gyrating fire rings around their hips.

"Cool!" Taylor exclaimed as one of the dancers tossed her hoop into the air, still burning, and then caught it. They stayed there watching the parade until most of the stilt walkers had gone by.

"Let's move over there," Keiko said, pointing to a clear place in the park with some benches, just a little ways away. "I really want to sit down."

"Me too," Taylor said, so they all drifted over to the benches.

"Want some?" a man on a blanket asked, holding up a bag.

Taylor jumped. She hadn't noticed him in the darkness. "No, thank you," she answered, giggling. He shrugged and they kept walking.

They sat down on the benches just as the fireworks began to start.

"Where did that guy on the blanket go?" Delilah asked. "He's disappeared."

Taylor scanned the crowd. "Oh, there he is," she said, looking across the street. "He's just getting into his car."

"Oh," Delilah said, bored.

They went back watching the fireworks, until Taylor said, "Hey, look! I guess that wasn't blanket guy's car."

Two policemen had come over, and the man was walking backwards. They could hear the police calling him back, but instead he picked up a plastic sword that someone had lost, and began running for the street — right behind Taylor!

"Go, go," Delilah yelled, laughing.

Taylor giggled. He made such a funny sight running towards them carrying that ridiculous sword. "Look, that guy over there is filming it," Taylor said.

The police came running after the man. One of them took a gadget out of his belt. Suddenly, the man fell right in front of them, twitching spastically. Taylor screamed. Delilah and Jessica ran to the man, along with the rest of the crowd. Taylor followed the girls. They were standing by the man, who was no longer moving. It looked like half the crowd was dialling 911. The police tried to get through, but the crowd kept pushing them back. Taylor started crying hysterically.

"Why won't anyone let the police through?" she shouted. "He needs help!"

"Honey, that's why we aren't letting those bastards at him," a woman said. "They tasered him."

"No, it's an overdose or something!" Taylor sobbed. "The police wouldn't do that!"

"Then why are they doing that?" the woman asked her, pointing at the policemen. They were arguing with a man at the side, and they snatched his cellphone. "He was filming it on his cell," the woman explained. "But it's okay, sweetie. It just makes them look more guilty. Half the crowd was filming that, and they can't delete all of it. Won't save that poor SOB though."

Just then, the ambulances came screeching in. The attendants had to fight their way through the crowd to reach the man. The boys and Anna, Grace, and Alexandra fought their way through the crowd towards Taylor and the girls.

"Omigod, did you guys see that happen?" Anna asked them. Taylor just became more hysterical.

"The police!" she sobbed. "And then … down! He just had a sword! I thought it was drugs."

Keiko put an arm around Taylor and led her back to the bench. The rest followed, in shock.

"I just can't believe that *our* police did that," Grace said. "What do they think they are, American?"

"Hey!" said Jonathon. "That was definitely your police who did it this time."

"Do you have your cell?" Keiko asked Taylor. Taylor didn't answer. She was still sobbing and incoherent. Keiko lifted Taylor's arm and searched through her jacket pockets. She found it and called Charlize. Jessica tried to give Taylor a Kleenex, but Taylor hit her away, burying her head in her hands, sobbing uncontrollably.

"Your mom is coming soon," Keiko told Taylor, patting her on the shoulder. Everybody else started phoning, too.

"We can drop you off at Mr. Yu's," Alexandra told Julian. "And you. At your home," she added to Tristan.

"There's Charlize," Keiko said with relief. Everyone looked up, happy to see a familiar adult.

"I was just coming to pick Taylor up anyway," Charlize said as she reached them, out of breath. "What happened? Oh, Taylor! Are you hurt?"

Taylor ignored her, still crying.

"Someone was shot … I mean tasered," said Keiko. "Not Taylor. This other guy … it was the police, it happened right next to us."

"Oh, baby," Charlize said, hugging Taylor. "Sweetie, please stop crying."

"She hasn't stopped crying since it happened," said Delilah.

"Oh no! She's probably in shock," Charlize said. "I'll have to take her to emergency for a tranquilizer." She coaxed Taylor along to the car and buckled her in her seat.

Chapter Seven

Alexandra Dunstan
Excited for Harbour with **Julian Reese** and **Tristan Patel**!

Alexandra went down the list, counting. "Three pictures of *tendu à la seconde*, head shots for all of them, four in *arabesque*, three letters of reference ..." she muttered.

Emma came into her room without knocking. "Mom wants to know if you want breakfast before you go to rehearsal."

"I'm not going to rehearsal right now, I'm going to Harbour and *then* rehearsal."

"Whatever," said Emma, raising her eyebrows and flopping onto Alexandra's bed. "How come you have so many black bodysuits out?"

Alexandra sighed. "I need to decide which one is best, so I know which one I am wearing for auditions."

"I like that one," Emma said, pointing at a black bodysuit laid on the pillow. Alexandra glared at her. That one was her favourite, but she didn't feel like agreeing with Emma right now.

"Go *away*, Emma."

"Aren't auditions after Christmas? How come you're getting ready now?" Emma showed no signs of leaving.

"Because I want to."

"Oh, okay. Do you want break—"

"Yes, go away!" Alexandra yelled. She pushed Emma out the door, shut the door behind her, and turned back to her computer. She sighed, looking at the pictures on the website. Crossing both fingers, she looked up. *Please, can I just get in somewhere and go. Royal Ballet School would be nice, but obviously SFB or SAB would be cool too. Really, I'm not that picky, any of the others would also be appreciated.*

Beth called upstairs, "Alexandra, if you want me to drive you downtown, we have to leave really soon. Get down here and eat breakfast."

Alexandra went downstairs, grabbing her bag. When she saw the waffles, she asked, "Actually, can I get something to eat downtown?"

"Alexandra.... Okay, I guess we don't really have time for you to eat here anyway." Alexandra grabbed a banana and followed her to the car.

As they drove downtown, Alexandra sang along to Linkin Park, "Hands held high into the sky so blue/The ocean opens up to swallow you."

"Is that the music from your contemporary solo?"

"No, Mom. I couldn't use it for a contemporary solo. I'm thinking of this one, though," she said switching the song. "Do you like it?"

"Yes, I like that one. Look over there. What are they protesting this time?"

Alexandra rolled her eyes. "It's called Flux."

"What, the protest?"

"No, the song." They pulled up to Harbour. Alexandra looked at her cellphone. She had enough time to go to Starbucks before Jules and Tristan got there. She ran across the street and ordered a Clean Green juice. When she looked out the window, Jules and Tristan had just arrived.

"Hey," she said as she reached them. "It's right here." Jules was looking around, confused.

"Wow, I was standing right in front of it," he said. "Is it really small?"

"No! It's upstairs, it's quite big actually."

"Geez, that's a lot of stairs," Julian said.

As they stretched in the studio, Julian asked, "Who's the dude in the pink girl's tights?"

"He's here a lot," Alexandra whispered. "He has mental problems. The government pays for his classes here. He's fine though."

The teacher came in, and Julian sat up quickly. "She's really tall," he sounded surprised, "and, like imposing-looking."

Tristan agreed. "She used to go to the academy, you know." He ran over to her.

"Come on," Alexandra said, grabbing Julian's arm.

"Hey! I'm so glad to see you guys," the teacher said, putting down her coffee and hugging Tristan and Alexandra. "And who is this?" she asked, smiling at Julian. "I'm Leah."

"That's Jules. He's new at the academy."

"Oh, I see. Don't listen to the academy too much, hey?"

"Okay!" Julian said, grinning.

"Well, let's start!" Leah addressed the whole room. There was a cheer and everyone moved onto the floor, shedding extra clothing and taking last swigs from their water bottles. Alexandra grabbed Julian's arm and led him to the centre. Tristan went to the very front, a bit to the left.

Leah interrupted the class twice to correct Julian's placement. "See?" she said to the class, one hand pushing his back in, the other pushing his stomach in, and her head shoving his ribs to one side. "When Jules finds this position, he is in a much more stable place. This will really improve your ballet, too. You'll really notice the difference in everything you do."

She finally moved on to across the floor exercises. "And five, six, seven, eight, and slide-brush-in-breathe … and one! Feel your back curve, and up — and fall. Alexandra, suspend — yes, that's right!" The class clapped and Alexandra grinned happily as she ran off. "Paul, you need to breathe, just fall. *And* jump! Five, six, and go —"

Julian grabbed his water bottle at the side of the room.

"So? Do you like it?" Tristan whispered excitedly. Julian nodded, choking on the water.

Alexandra ran over to them. "Jules! You're really good at jazz. Come across the floor with me?"

"Sure," Julian said, concentrating on not hiccupping. Tristan glared at him. "Why don't we go as a three?"

"Sure," said Alexandra, smiling and taking Julian's arm. "Come on, we can go in the next group." They joined with a girl in brightly coloured Lululemon tights, forcing Tristan to go in the group after.

"Good energy, Julian!" Leah called.

"I really like this class!" Julian whispered excitedly as they walked to the other corner. "I'm totally stoked to come again."

"Yeah, let's come again without Lexi."

"What?" Julian was puzzled.

"Nothing. Come, quick — we can go in this group." He shoved Julian ahead of him.

"Okay," said Julian. They danced across the floor without Alexandra.

After class, they got changed quickly, so they wouldn't be late for rehearsal. As soon as they'd left the changing room, Tristan walked quickly for the stairs, tossing a sunny "Bye-bye!" to the lady at the desk.

"Hey, Tristan," Julian said, interrupting his chattering about how great the class had been for the first time. "Alexandra's still getting changed."

Tristan stopped walking. Alexandra came out a couple seconds later, and they all went downstairs together. Julian couldn't stop talking about how cool Leah, in particular, and Harbour, in general, were, and Alexandra easily gushed about both of them with him. Tristan tolerated this for about two blocks, but then he'd had enough and interrupted them.

"I bet Leah would choreograph a solo for you for competition, if you asked her."

Julian immediately stopped walking and turned to him. "Do you think so? That would be friggin' awesome!"

"Yeah, sure. She's done loads for me."

"She did one for me last year," Alexandra said. Julian did a happy little skippity hop.

"Okay, stop that," Tristan said. They reached the academy and went to get changed. Tristan smirked at Alexandra as he followed Julian into the boys' changing room. She rolled her eyes and went off to to the girls'.

"Dmitri's coming to rehearsal today," Grace announced to the washroom at large.

"Good," Aiko said, smiling as she fixed her bun. "I am happy to finally rehearse with him! I was beginning to wonder if the first time would be on stage."

Alexandra scooted in between the two of them to put her hair up.

"How come you're so late?" Grace asked. Alexandra shrugged. "You should get here early. You know how much Mr. Moretti yelled at you last time. I just don't want you to get yelled at again. You should probably go over his corrections before we go in. Do you want me to help you?"

Alexandra stuck hair pins in her mouth just before Grace finished speaking, and then mimed that she was too busy with her hair to answer.

"Okay, okay. I was just trying to help." Grace left to go upstairs. And the rest of the girls quickly followed.

In the hallway, Dmitri was sitting on one of the chairs, everyone in a semi-circle around him. He was not tall, or skinny (in fact, he was a bit chubby for a dancer) and he was rather lazy. He was tolerated because he was strong, and also because the company was always short of male dancers. He rarely bathed, believing that body spray worked just as well as water, and laughed if anyone complained (he also thought that not bathing proved he was straight). And he was scary to do *pas* with, since he liked to threaten to drop girls as they were in the air. Dmitri also liked to amuse himself by waiting until the very last second to catch his partner and experimenting with using only one or no hands to partner. Nobody *really* wanted to work with him, but he was in the company, so they all tried to, just for the status of it.

"I like to dance balls out," Dmitri was saying as Alexandra came and joined them.

"So — no dance belt?" Anna joked.

Dmitri looked at her. "You think you'd like it if I dance with no dance belt?" Anna shook her head, but Dmitri ignored her. "Okay, maybe you'd like it like this?" He stood up and swung his hips all around. "I have no problem with that."

"I don't think that it's that large," Grace said drily, making sure that Dmitri couldn't hear her. Alexandra grimaced. Dmitri was wearing white knit tights that were so old that they were completely see-through. He always wore them over nothing but his skin coloured dance belt. To complete the effect, he would roll the tights and the dance belt together, down over his hips, so you could see way more of his butt than anyone wanted. Not to mention that his white shirt was too short for him, and stopped quite a bit before his tights, giving everyone a good view of his belly. He, of course, was under the impression that this made him irresistible. No one seemed to agree.

Mr. Yu came out and called Grace, Dmitri, Tristan, and Aiko into the studio. He slapped Dmitri on the back fondly as he entered the studio. "No drunk today?

Anna, Alexandra, Leon, and Jonathon were left waiting for Mr. Moretti in silence. Just when Alexandra thought she couldn't stand the quiet anymore, Mr. Moretti called them in. Alexandra tried to avoid eye contact with Mr. Moretti.

"Today will be good for you, boys," Mr. Moretti said. Leon and Jonathon groaned.

"Now, babies," Mr. Moretti continued, ignoring Leon and Jonathon. "This must be sexy. I mean it, babies. If it is not sexy, I will kick you out. Go to your room, close the door, and practice in front of the mirror. It must have fire, passion." He taught them the first bit. "No, no! Alexandra, you move like you are very, very shy. It must be sexy, baby. Practice in front of the mirror, look at yourself. No, no, now you just move your hipses. You are not doing hip hop, you must be slow, controlled. And *move*, and move ... like honey, molasses. You think you are the most beautiful woman in the world. Now you hide your face, but not because you are shy. Because you still know that the man is watching you ... yes. Anna, now look up and see if it is working ... yes."

Jonathon laughed and imitated them on the side.

"Look, even the one without a brain can be sexier than you, Alexandra! You must work baby, you really must work."

Alexandra bit her lip and nodded, trying to do it better.

"All right boys ... now we will work on the lifts, yes? All right, you enter, both boys carrying the girl ... Anna, you try first. Leon downstage, Jonathon upstage ... yes.

Now, Anna, you come on sitting on their shoulders. Yes, arms like this. Leon, don't drop the girl! Lower Anna down gently, she is your princess, you are a slave, do you want to be executed? Yes … now walk slowly down the centre … the corps are here, and here, ignore them, they are your slaves, they are like the furniture. Now Anna, the part we worked on last day … yes, *hold* the arabesque … now, Jonathon you pick her up like this … Leon, you stand here and present, be ready … Now start walking back Jonathon, Leon, take her hand … now lower her down. No, not like a sack of potatoes! She must stay in the arabesque, tilt her more forward. Anna, hold your stomach, baby. Alexandra! Are you paying attention? Because I will not be happy if I have to waste time going over this again. Now we will try it with the music."

He walked over and started to fiddle with the CD player. They heard the music for Spanish choreography, and the boys began dancing. Mr. Moretti swore and tried again, getting Chinese. Jonathon and Leon happily jumped the Chinese jumps.

"Having fun?" Mr. Moretti called out angrily, not turning around. He swore again and began muttering in Italian. "Where did the Arabian music go? It was right in between here and here."

"Maybe Mr. Yu accidentally erased it?" Jonathon suggested.

"Why would that man have done that? No, don't tell me, I don't want to know." Mr. Moretti tossed the CD case down on the table. "I believe you. Now you will just have to hear me singing. Have fun, children. From the beginning please, Anna still."

Alexandra tried to mark the choreography on the side, but it was hard to mark choreography that was mostly highly stylized *pas de deux* work. She smirked; Anna's back was completely red from Leon and Jonathon sliding her down wrong. They all suddenly stopped, as they heard Mr. Yu yelling in the next room. Mr. Moretti glared furiously at the wall that divided the two studios. "Shall we try it again?"

When the rehearsal was almost over, Mr. Moretti looked at his watch. There were two minutes left. "Alexandra, now you try," he announced, smiling his Cheshire cat smile. Alexandra drew a deep breath and walked over to Jonathon and Leon, who were groaning in mock pain.

"All right, from the beginning, with Alexandra. Five ... six ... seven, eight, *and* ... No, Alexandra hold yourself! Try again. Fine, just continue. I can't watch that anymore." Mr. Moretti folded his arms. He didn't bother singing, and the silence was overpowering. When they finished, they all stood awkwardly in the centre of the room.

"Are you finished?" Mr. Moretti asked, sounding pained. Alexandra nodded, blushing. She began to wiggle her feet around nervously. "I will not let anything like that go on stage. You were obviously not watching. When you are in the studio, I am God. Do you understand me? When you are outside of the studio you may do whatever you wish, but here I am God and you must obey me. If I say do something, you do it. Exactly how

I said. And pay attention the entire time. Okay, everybody may go home."

Anna burst into giggles as soon as they reached the stairs. "Omigod, that was hilarious!" Wait 'til I tell Grace, she'll love that one. That was totally classic Mr. Moretti. 'I am God ...'" Alexandra felt sick. She rushed to get changed. She wanted to get out of the academy before everyone else got out of rehearsal.

As she trudged up the stairs she stopped to look at a framed photo of Leonie Camden on the wall. The Demidovskis framed pictures and news clippings of their favourite graduates on the wall, and she was one of Alexandra's favourites. Leonie graduated four years ago, and she had accomplished everything that Alexandra dreamed of. Leonie got her RAD Solo Seal award at sixteen, and she was always chosen for solo and principal roles. After winning gold at the Prix de Lausanne during her graduation year, Leonie was invited to join the San Francisco Ballet.

Alexandra smiled to herself, looking at the picture of Leonie in *arabesque*. It was taken right after she won gold. Leonie looked exhausted but happy as she posed in her tutu. Alexandra had watched Leonie perform that variation on YouTube a million times. She always imagined herself in Leonie's place, trying to feel the way Leonie's muscles worked during the harder parts, the way the lights would appear, the size and rake of the stage....

Alexandra continued up the stairs. Her resolve was back.

"Alexa! Alexandra!" Mrs. Demidovski had spotted her from inside the office and called her in. "Come here, eh?" She gestured at a chair.

"Hello, Mrs. Demidovski," Alexandra said nervously. She walked quickly into the office and sat down, twisting her hands nervously in her lap.

"Where is your coat? You need coat go outside, it is cold! I don't want everyone get sick before *The Nutcracker*, cannot be some fever, some cough, some something else."

"I've got a coat right here." Alexandra held it up for inspection.

"Ah. It doesn't look warm enough, eh?"

"It's warm."

"Ah that's good. So, you have lots of friends here? Grace? Grace is good girl, good friend for you. Also new boy, what is name ... Mr. Demidovski like? Julie?"

"Julian?"

"Yes, yes. Good boy, nice body. And Tristan, work hard, much improve." She started chuckling at the idea of Tristan. "You're a good girl, much improve. Don't worry, just work, eh? Get stronger, then more roles, okay? Must fight, be strong. Sometimes there is tree, a little cherry tree, have pretty blossoms ... it is growing, watered ... but then an axe come, *whack!*" Mrs. Demidovski hands were like knives as she mimed chopping the little tree into bits. "Chop, chop ... must not be like this, must be strong, too hard to chop down. And if axe come, chop, must grow back, stronger. Cherries come. Yes? You need something, come talk to Mrs. Demidovski."

"Okay. Thank you, Mrs. Demidovski." Alexandra felt absurdly elated.

Mrs. Demidovski sat back; the conversation was clearly finished. Alexandra stood up, nodded, and smiled awkwardly, thanking her again.

As Alexandra walked toward her mom's car, the happiness she had felt from Mrs. Demidovski's words slowly evaporated as common sense kicked in. It was alright for Mrs. Demidovski to say "be a good girl, work hard, wait," but Alexandra had been waiting and working ever since she came to the academy. *Grace and Anna never had to wait, and they hadn't even won a bronze,* Alexandra fumed. *I am just so tired of the whole academy!*

"Hey, how was rehearsal?" Beth asked as Alexandra got in the car.

"Hell, as usual. I seriously hate Mr. Moretti," Alexandra said, pulling her *pointe* shoes out and placing them on the car cup holders.

"Alexandra, put those away! They stink!"

"They're wet! If I leave them in my bag they'll just stay wet, and then they'll melt, and then they'll be dead and I'll have to use a new pair tomorrow."

"All right, fine. But put them on the back seat."

"Fine. Oh, and Mrs. Demidovski randomly called me into her office after rehearsal."

"For what?"

"The usual. Be a good girl, everything will be all right. Don't worry, work hard …"

"How nice of her." Beth's tone was sarcastic. "Just to make sure we keep paying her, I suppose."

"I don't think so, actually. You know how awkward she is about money. I don't really understand her. I swear, it's like Mr. and Mrs. Demidovski really like me every time they talk to me, and then casting comes up and I don't know what happens." Alexandra winced. "Ow! I need ice ... and Tylenol."

"Tylenol? I don't like you taking it so often."

"Mom, my ankle's killing me."

"Okay, but be sure. I don't want you ODing on Tylenol."

Alexandra started giggling. "I can totally see that in *24 Hours*: 'Ballet Dancer Teen Overdoses on Tylenol.'"

"Alexandra! It's not funny."

In her room, Alexandra heaved her bag onto the bed with a groan. She took her school books out; biology, *Hamlet*, history.... A paper fell out of her English binder. It was a letter from McKinley inviting any Super Achievers students to submit their accomplishments to be posted on the wall and in the student newsletter. Underneath was a reminder to register if you wanted to perform at the school assembly.

Alexandra sat down on her bed and stared at the paper, biting her lip as she considered. Bronze at the Genees might be considered good by the kids at the academy, but she knew that the others in the Super Achievers program would just want to know why not a gold. A girl in her class had made the gymnastics team for the Olympics, and one of the boys had just missed school because he had a special violin solo performance in New York. Katy had just got back from three months of modelling in Italy. And she hadn't seen Josh or Emily in weeks because they were filming. *And that's just the things I know about,* Alexandra thought, pushing her textbooks off the bed so that they fell to the floor with a crash.

"And as for the assembly performance? Forget it!" She said out loud to her history book. The rhythmic gymnasts would steal the show, like they did every year, and the Evergreen Arts dancers would embarrass themselves by performing, which they did every year and never seemed to realize. No, performing was *not* an option. Especially if Diana was going to perform. Diana was in the program for opera, and she was incredible. Alexandra groaned and lay on her back, staring at the ceiling. She clenched her hands into fists and punched the pillow. *If I'd just gotten gold ... but I still wouldn't have performed, I guess.* Ballet couldn't compete for coolness with rhythmic gymnastics and opera, and she couldn't risk the fallout if people didn't think she was any good. She couldn't endure the embarrassment.

"Alexandra! Dinnertime soon, come and set the table," Beth called.

"Coming," Alexandra yelled back. She sighed, feeling her jaw line and cheeks. It didn't seem possible to just stop. She needed to. She would be perfectly fine, and then suddenly everything would seem too much, she would panic stuff food into her body as fast as she could. It didn't have to be a lot, just fast. And then, she would have to throw it up. She couldn't dance on a full stomach, it wasn't possible. Throwing up made her feel so much better. It calmed her down, made her feel like she was succeeding, even if everything seemed out of control. She could walk out of the bathroom and not feel so inferior, and for a couple minutes nothing mattered so much. It was worth it, just for that feeling. *But I have to stop doing it so often,* Alexandra thought as she felt her face. *What is the point if it makes my face bigger?*

She sighed and turned on her laptop. Immediately a message from Jules popped up.

Alexandra Dunstan

Julian Reese
Hey

Alexandra Dunstan
Hey, 'sup?

Julian Reese
Um, nothing. Do you have Leah's number?

Alexandra Dunstan
Ya ...wait a sec

Alexandra Dunstan
778–448–2053 is her cell

Alexandra Dunstan
She runs Movement Conspiracy, u can google them

Julian Reese
Thx!

Alexandra Dunstan
No prob

Alexandra Dunstan
How was RAD?

Julian Reese
Uh...rlly bad

Julian Reese
Haha! Always

Julian Reese
Was rehearsal good?

Alexandra Dunstan
It was ok...

Alexandra Dunstan
Gotta go for dinner, see u tmw

Julian Reese
K, good night

Alexandra Dunstan
'night

Alexandra smiled, looking at the blank screen. *Jules is rather sweet ...*

Emma burst angrily into the room. "Mom said that *you* had to set the table. I did it yesterday; you have to do it today." Alexandra ignored her.

"I'm not doing it!" whined Emma.

"Fine! Just be quiet and go away!"

Alexandra went downstairs and began setting the table.

Chapter Eight

Julian Reese

"I, I wish you could swim — Like the dolphins, like dolphins can swim — Though nothing, nothing will keep us together ... We can beat them, forever and ever...!"

Julian woke up and reached to turn off his alarm clock. It wasn't there. But it continued to beep. He realized that, somehow, he was facing the wrong way. He flipped, reached blearily for the alarm-off button, then flopped back down on the bed and closed his eyes with relief at the silence. He lay there for a second, psyching himself up, then managed to jolt himself out of bed. He yawned as he felt his legs clench. *Too many classes.* It was five o'clock, way too early to be conscious, but Mr. Yu was making him do school shows with the youth company because they needed another boy. So he was going to some random elementary school to perform. He yawned again and stumbled into his clothes.

Mrs. Yu had gotten up even earlier and made break-fast. Julian was confused. He had assumed that they would just eat cereal, like usual. He looked across at the girls, but they just shrugged. He sat down and took his plate, wondering what the mound of greasy, white, slightly burnt food was exactly. He prodded it with his fork, running a list of possibilities through his head:

Fritter? Pancake? Dumpling? He tried a bit. All he tasted was oil, held together by flour. He spat it out in a napkin.

"It's last night's dumplings," Mrs. Yu said. "Mash, is pancake. You try." Julian was horrified. He hadn't liked the dumplings the first time around, and he was sure that he'd puke if he tried them a second time. The girls started giggling and handed their plates back to Mrs. Yu.

"What's wrong? You don't want breakfast?"

Julian handed back his plate, too. "It's just kinda too early for breakfast." His stomach growled, and he wondered if he had any energy bars in his room.

"Okay, okay. If you don't want breakfast, tell me before I get up and make!"

Julian followed the girls out into the hall. "Do you guys have any food?"

Keiko giggled and said, "You should eat Mrs. Yu's breakfast, if you're so hungry."

Mao nodded, grinning. "Then you grow very tall, and not get sick," she imitated Mrs. Yu.

"Just gimme some food? Please?" Julian pleaded. They went into Mao's room, and Keiko went to grab some of her stash too. They spread it out on the bed.

"Hurry up," Keiko said. "We have to get ready for the show, and I don't want leave you here with my food."

Julian grinned at her and made his selection. He thanked the girls before leaving with the food under his shirt.

As soon as he was ready, Julian went out into the kitchen. Mr. Yu was already there, eating his breakfast. Julian watched him in amazement. He didn't even seem to taste what he was eating. Suddenly he stood up and said, "Okay, go now."

Everyone trudged after him to the van and shoved into the vehicle, trying to make room among all the costumes.

"Where are we going?" Julian whispered to Keiko as they headed downtown.

"To the academy to pick up everyone else," Keiko whispered back. Julian groaned. Of course, the other dancers needed a ride. But it seemed like an impossible number of people to fit in the van. The others got into the van with a chorus of "*Ohayou*," and "'Morning," and then they all lapsed into silence.

When they finally got to the school, a custodian let them into the gym where they would be performing. Everybody started stripping down to their dance clothes and putting on their warm-ups. Julian stopped moving.

"What's wrong?" Kageki asked curiously, noticing Julian's horrified expression.

"I forgot my warm-ups. And my non-costume dance clothes!"

Kageki laughed. "Sorry, man, that sucks," he said, trying to be sympathetic. "I write a list of everything I need to bring every day, and then I check it all off," he told Julian as they both went to get chairs to use as a *barre*.

"What? Like, everything?"

"Yes, everything. Cellphone, dance belt, lunch, pencils ..."

"You are *really* weird," Julian said shaking his head. Kageki grinned. He didn't deny it.

Mr. Yu yelled, "Hurry!" impatiently, and began to leading the exercises before they had finished setting up their chairs. Julian reached down to hold his chair and realized that it wasn't going to be any help at all. It was way too short and light to support him. He moved over to the wall and tried to find a surface that he could grip onto. It was all very smooth, so he gave up and just touched the wall lightly to get his balance. He tried to stand in first position in preparation for the exercise as Mr. Yu tried to find a good piece of music, but his feet immediately slid out of position on the slippery floor. He looked over at Tristan and Kageki, who just smirked at him.

"Got any rosin?" he asked hopefully.

"Nope," Kageki said, looking forward as Mr. Yu glared at him.

"Sprinkle some water on the floor," Tristan whispered.

"I forgot my water bottle," Julian whispered back. Tristan rolled his eyes and passed his over.

When Julian was done sprinkling the floor, Tristan happily grabbed his bottle from Julian and started to spray the rest of the floor, too.

"Ahh! Too much!" Aiko wailed, as Kageki narrowly missed splashing her *pointe* shoes.

"Enough," Mr. Yu said impatiently. They all went back to their chairs and walls, the girls glaring at the boys as they attempted to avoid the puddles of water and grumbled about it ruining their *pointe* shoes. They got through *pliés* without incident. Mr. Yu actually just stood there, staring into space, as they did the exercise.

He snapped out of it and started to give a *tendu* exercise, but stopped suddenly and ordered them to take their clothes off. They groaned and began shedding layers. They did the rest of the *barre* in a hurry and had no centre practice as Mr. Yu suddenly realized what time it was. The second they finished, they changed into their costumes in a panic, and the girls began fixing their *pointe* shoes and trying to warm their feet up a bit more. The boys went into the centre of the gym and began testing out their pirouettes.

"I love this floor!" Julian said as he went around five times. "It's so awesomely slippery!"

"Yeah, but wait till jumps," Tristan said. He turned six times and then fell on his side, one hand on his chest, the other stretching to the sky.

"Bet I can do seven!" Kageki said.

"Bet you can't," Tristan said. Julian and Tristan watched as Kageki prepared, and then just as he started Tristan yelled, "Jinx!"

Kageki gave up on doing a proper pirouette and turned into a spiralling spin, both hands clutched onto his heart. "I hate you," he informed Tristan and prepared again.

"Don't wind up," Tristan said, laughing at him. Kageki stopped, looked at Tristan, and then prepared with exaggerated care. He went around one ... two ... three ... four ... five ... he started slowing down at six, but just as he was about to stop, he twisted his body and managed to get around another time.

"Nice!" Julian said admiringly.

"Cheater," Tristan said. "Now me." He did the first three pirouettes normally, then hunched his shoulders and grabbed his crotch for four more.

"It doesn't count if you do it that way," Kageki argued. But Tristan defended himself.

Julian did a few pirouettes off to the side. He could do five max, grabbing his crotch or no.

The show went pretty well as far as Julian could tell. The children liked the national dances, tolerated the waltz and contemporary dances, yawned through Aiko and Dmitri's *pas de deux* from *Le Corsaire*, and were wildly enthusiastic about Tristan, Julian, and Kageki's version of the Russian dance taken from *The Nutcracker*.

"I need a drink," Dmitri said later, as everyone unloaded themselves and the costumes out of the car.

"Me too," Julian said. Dmitri looked at him in surprise.

"We have costume fittings today," Tristan reminded him.

"You want to go to No. 5?" Dmitri asked Mr. Yu.

He nodded, continuing to unload. Everyone began to go inside, but Mr. Yu called the boys back to help.

"Where's No. 5?" Julian asked, as they pulled out a trunk of costumes.

"Downtown. It's a good bar," Dmitri told him.

"No it's not," Tristan said quietly, wrinkling his nose in disgust. "It just has strippers,"

"You want to come with us?" Dmitri asked Julian, ignoring Tristan.

"Sure!" Julian said. "Uh, actually I can't. I don't have any I.D."

Love You, Hate You

Dmitri grimaced. "Too bad, man. You find some I.D. and I'll take you. They used to have Pam Anderson stripping there before she got famous."

"No, it was Courtney Love," Mr. Yu said. "Come on, let's go."

Dmitri rolled his eyes and whispered "Pam!" to Julian. He got in the van and they drove away, leaving Julian, Tristan, and Kageki to carry the costumes into the academy.

The whole hall was filled with people waiting to get into the studio, which was full of precariously stacked tutus and large props. As Tristan and Julian walked by carrying a trunk, a peculiar man, who was measuring Taylor's hips, called out to them. "Boys! Hurry back, I need you next. So nice to see you again, Tristan."

"Who was *that*?" Julian asked.

"The costume guy." Tristan was struggling as they manoeuvred the trunk down the stairs. "His name is Cromwell Gilly. He used to go to McKinley. He's training to be a designer now, and he likes to practice sewing and stuff at the academy." They heaved the trunk down onto the costume-room floor with relief. "Whew! Let's leave the rest for Leon and Jonathon, okay?"

"Sounds good to me," Julian said, and they trudged up the stairs.

Cromwell Gilly was even more eccentric close up. He was very small and had long, thin blond hair, and he was in constant motion. He wore extremely tight, black skinny pants, pointed leather shoes, a white poet's shirt open to show a great deal of his chest, a belt with a huge

135

silver buckle on it, three rings, and a leather and silver necklace. As he darted around measuring people, he'd tell them to put their arms up and down, then shout out their measurements to Michael's mother, and generally promoting noise and confusion. The students were sprawled all over the hall, talking loudly to be heard over the commotion.

"By the way, he likes to be called by his full name," Tristan whispered to Julian.

"He's even more *interesting* with sound," Julian whispered to Tristan as soon as they were close enough to hear him. They both sat down on the floor next to Alexandra, snickering.

"Oh. My. God." Cromwell Gilly said as he measured Aiko's ankle.

"What?" she asked, sounding worried.

"Oh nothing, nothing," he said, frowning. He called out the number to Michael's mother, his eyebrows raised. She gave him a weird look, but wrote down the number.

"What? What?" Aiko asked, starting to freak out.

"Oh, nothing," Michael's mother said.

"Done!" Cromwell Gilly sang out, smiling at Aiko. She walked off frowning, clenching and unclenching her hands. "Lexi, baby, how are you, love?" he asked Alexandra, gesturing her forward. Without letting her answer, he continued. "I can't believe I was called in this late. What were *they* thinking?" Cromwell Gilly didn't like the Demidovskis. Every year he would design new costumes for them, and every year they would nod politely and continue using the twenty- or thirty-year-old costumes instead. Any time something on the building was fixed, he took it as evidence that they had money they could give him to make the costumes but preferred to waste it on stupid things like fixing the roof.

"Did you know that they got a new car?" he asked ALexandra in a stage whisper as he measured her hips. She shook her head. "Done!" he said, spinning her around by the shoulder and pushing her away.

"Next!" Angela stepped forward, and Cromwell Gilly frowned. "What are *you* in?" he asked, scanning his list. "Oh, 'Trepak,'" he answered himself in relief. "Thank god it's not a tutu! Those 'Trepak' dresses are easy to let out." Behind her Alexandra and Tristan giggled. Angela's face turned completely red. Cromwell Gilly gestured her away, saying "We'll just do you later, shall we? Next!" Delilah giggled as she stepped forward.

"Del, darling, how are you! What *are* we going to do about your boobage m'dear?" he said, frowning as he measured them. Delilah blushed. "We'll just take some of the material from the waist and add it to the chest, shall we?" She rolled her eyes and he called for the next dancer.

Tristan shoved Julian forward. But, much to Julian's relief, Cromwell Gilly didn't have anything embarrassing to say about him, merely remarking that he had "a very nice body for dance, don't you think, Tristan?"

In the big room where the stacks of costumes were, the girls were rummaging through the tutus, each trying to find one in their size. Taylor was trying to do up Kaitlyn's Clara costume, but it wasn't working. Kaitlyn looked like she was about to cry, as Taylor gave up happily and said, loudly, "It's just not going to do up, Kaitlyn. It's all right, though. They always have to adjust the costumes for me, too, because I'm so small. Like, in width."

Keiko found a tutu that fit. But she scowled when she looked at the tag, and went off to find another one.

"Are some of them taken already?" Julian asked Tristan.

"No, it's just that these tutus are so old, they kind of have history, you know? Everyone wants to get one that a good dancer, or one with a good body type used to wear, just to see if it fits. It's kind of cool that they used to wear it. So you always look inside the costume to see who wore it before you."

"Yeah," Kageki said enthusiastically. "I got to wear a costume that Mr. Yu wore once. It was so cool...."

"It fit you?" Julian asked.

Tristan laughed. "No, duh! They took it up like 50 percent."

"But I still wore it," Kageki said defensively.

Suddenly, they heard Taylor say, "But I got it first!" She sounded close to tears.

Jessica was trying to pry her tutu away from her, saying "I *need* to wear that one! I'm taller than you. Go find one that a shorter person wore."

Keiko came up to Taylor holding a tutu. "Taylor, try this one. It's small, and Leonie wore it!"

"Leonie Camden?" Taylor excitedly shoved the other tutu into Jessica's arms. She tried it on and Keiko did her up.

"It'll need to be taken in," Keiko said.

"No, it's fine," Taylor said. She shot Jessica a worried glance to make sure she wasn't trying to steal this tutu also. "This is so cool! Can you *believe* that Leonie did this dance once? I mean seriously," she shook her head. "Thank you *so* much, Keiko!" She hugged her.

"Can we go, yet, do you think?" Julian asked. He was getting bored and ripping apart tape that held the floor pieces together.

"Yes," Kageki said.

"Don't we have a speech thingy from the Demidovskis today?" Tristan asked, turning to Kageki.

"No. The Demidovskis decided that they didn't want to come today."

"Figures," said Tristan. "Come on, let's get out of here fast, before anyone decides they need us." He ushered Kageki and Julian down the hall as fast as he could.

"Where are you guys going?" Alexandra asked as Michael's mother hooked her into a tutu.

"Outta here, loser!" Tristan said, laughing.

"Loser yourself!" Alexandra stuck out her tongue at him.

As they got changed, Julian asked Tristan and Kageki if they wanted to hang out.

"I *want* to," Tristan said, "but I have so much physics homework and an in-class English essay tomorrow."

"Okay, I will," Kageki said, shrugging.

Julian felt a bit awkward as he and Kageki walked out together. They didn't normally hang out without Tristan. "So, where do you want to go?"

"I don't really want to go anywhere, I'm too tired," Kageki said. "Could we just go to your homestay? I love going to Mr. Yu's. My homestay is so weird. My homestay mom gets really mad if people come over and I haven't asked her like a week before."

"Sure," Julian shrugged. "Come on, that's our bus!" He broke into a run.

As they walked up the street to Mr. Yu's house, they talked about the weirdo on the bus who'd been giving out religious pamphlets and talking about Armageddon.

"Guess what, Kageki. The world's going to end tomorrow!" Kageki rolled his eyes. "What religion do you have mostly in Japan?"

"Um … well, Buddhism and Christianity. But the Christians are more here, of course. So basically, in Japan, this is most common," he shaped his hands into the sign of prayer with his fingers out stretched, "and here is more this," he made the sign of prayer with his fingers crossed over each other.

"Cool," Julian said, making both signs. "My mom's Buddhist."

"Really?" Kageki sounded surprised. "How come you didn't know that already then?"

"I don't live with her. With Satya."

"You call your mom by her name?" Kageki asked as he followed Julian into his room.

"Yeah," Julian shrugged. "It's her name, right? She says she wants to be addressed as a person, not as a role."

"Okay…?"

"Her full name is actually Satyagraha." Julian flipped open his laptop and signed onto Facebook. "Look, here she is."

"Mmm … she's kissing that woman!" Kageki said. "Does your mom … like girls?" He leaned forward to take a closer look at Satya's profile picture.

"Um, she likes both," Julian explained awkwardly. "Look …" He searched for another picture. "This is her boyfriend Luigi. He's awesome. I got a scholarship from the Demidovskis for tuition at the academy, but I still had to pay homestay fees, and he paid them."

"But … he's not your father?"

"No, he's been with Satya for less than a year," Julian said, switching pages. "This is my dad, Will … and my half-brother River, and his mom, my dad's girlfriend, Daisy."

Kageki stared at the picture, puzzlement creasing his face.

Julian flopped onto his bed after dinner and phoned Will.

"Hey," he said, trying to keep his voice down. The walls were so thin that everyone could hear him if he used his normal voice.

"Hey, how are you? Daisy's just out taking River to his soccer practice, but you can call later if you want to talk to him."

"No, I wanted to talk to you, Will. I need to know if you want to come to the performance or not."

"Well, Jules, I don't really know. It depends on your grandparents … I'm not sure if they are going to buy us tickets."

"But they're not coming, right?"

"No. I'll get Daisy to phone them tomorrow."

"They're your parents, you should call them," Julian pointed out. "Anyway, goodnight Will. Love you."

"Sure thing, buddy," Will said. He hung up.

Chapter Nine

Kaitlyn Wardle
Really happy to be having RAD class again tomorrow!!

Kaitlyn tucked her essay into her bag, the mark facing in so no one could see it.

"Bus pass?" the driver asked, stopping her. She blushed, got it out, and made her way to the back of the bus. No one else from the academy was on the bus. *Weird,* she thought. *I didn't think I was catching the later bus.* Kaitlyn looked out the window and saw Michael and Chloe come flying down the street to the bus. The driver opened the doors again and waited for them.

"Where's everybody else?" Kaitlyn asked when they'd sat down next to her. "Are we catching a different bus?"

"No, they all got a ride with Anna," Chloe said as she unpacked her lunch.

"Her mom picked her up from school today," Michael elaborated. "I guess they just didn't have enough seats for you. Yum, can I have one?" he asked Chloe as she got out her baby carrots. She held the bag out to him. "Aren't you eating any lunch, Kaitlyn?"

"I'm not hungry," Kaitlyn said, turning and looking out the window.

"Are you sure?" asked Chloe and held out her bag of carrots. "You can have some of these if you want."

"We're just concerned about you," Michael added.

"I'm fine," Kaitlyn answered sharply, sending them a look that was scary enough to shut them up. "We have RAD class today right?"

"Yeah, we've got Mrs. Mallard," Michael answered. "You've had her before, right?"

"Yeah. She's coached me on all of my exams. I think she's going to put me through my Solo Seal this year. "

"Wow, you're doing that really young," said Michael. "Even Leonie didn't do it when she was that young."

"I know," Kaitlyn said with a smug little giggle. She pulled out a Ziploc bag of trail mix.

"Oh, so you *are* eating lunch," Chloe said with an exaggerated tone of relief. Kaitlyn glared at her.

Kaitlyn got off the bus and moved quickly toward the academy, putting enough distance between herself and Michael and Chloe that no one could accuse her of being with them.

Everyone was sitting in the hallway eating and stretching. Tristan was munching on a sandwich, chewing exaggeratedly, facing one of the security cameras. "Look at me! I'm eating bread!" he told the camera, pointing at the sandwich in his hands and opening his mouth wide. "I think I might have a Coke next!" Alexandra, Delilah, Grace, and Jessica giggled at him. They kept their lunches out of sight of the security camera, though.

"Where's Angela?" Jessica asked.

"I dunno," Delilah said and shrugged.

"Who cares?" Anna asked, laughing. "I wish she'd just go away and never come back!"

"She looks like a horse, but ugly and fat!" Alexandra chimed in.

"No, she looks more like a groundhog," Grace said.

"I think she's half and half," Tristan said, turning his attention away from the camera. "The size of a horse, and the brain and body type of a wart hog."

"Nice," Anna said, laughing. Kaitlyn nervously walked past them, trying not to attract their attention. But she couldn't escape Anna's notice. "Oh, look who finally got here."

"Yep," said Kaitlyn, giving her a sweet smile. She went to get changed, quickly, before they could say anything else.

When she came upstairs again, everyone was still sitting in the same place. There was no free floor space, but there was a free chair so she took it. Keiko came upstairs just as Kaitlyn sat down. She rose out of her chair, hoping to go sit with Keiko, but she went to sit on the stairs with a bunch of the lower level students. Kaitlyn sat down again then immediately shot to her feet with a shriek. Delilah had slipped her pasta onto the seat, and Kaitlyn had sat right on it.

"Why did you do that?" Everybody started to laugh as they got a good view of Kaitlyn's sauce-covered butt.

"Oh, my God, you like just ruined my lunch! Now what am I supposed to eat?" Delilah feigned outrage.

"Yeah, you should totally buy her a new lunch,"

Tristan piped up, trying not to snigger. "That was really mean of you to ruin her lunch."

Kaitlyn burst into tears and ran downstairs, and a fresh wave of smothered laughter followed her.

"What's her problem?" Alexandra said.

"So sensitive," Grace said, shaking her head sorrowfully.

Fortunately Kaitlyn had an extra uniform bodysuit and tights in her locker She couldn't stop crying as she changed into them. *What right does Delilah have to make fun of me?* She tried to calm down and stop the tears. Only the mental image of what her face must look like enabled her to stop bawling, and she slowly started to breathe normally. She felt her face to try and judge exactly how puffy it had gotten. Taking deep breaths, she gathered her courage to leave the bathroom stall and checked the crack between the door and the wall. Luckily no one was there. She went to the mirror and attempted to make her face look normal with liberal amounts of cold water and toilet paper. As soon as she felt she looked as good as she was going to be able to look, she forced herself to walk out.

The RAD Advanced II class was the highest level offered as a group class, so it was always packed. Kaitlyn got upstairs just as everyone was filing into the studio. She didn't feel up for the usual race and slide for a good spot at the *barre*, so she resigned herself to a spot at the back.

"Oh, Kaitlyn!" trilled Mrs. Mallard as she turned and saw her. "It's always such a pleasure to have you in class, my dear. Are you excited to learn the Solo Seal work?" She lowered her voice to a stage whisper. "I think you'll really enjoy it. It's quite different from the previous syllabus work, much more focused on musicality and performance. Of course, the technical work is quite challenging, but I'm quite confident that you will be more than capable in that area. I was discussing it with Mrs. Demidovski just the other day, and we both agreed that you were quite up to the challenge."

"Yes, I'm really excited," Kaitlyn said, trying to sound enthusiastic while realizing that everyone else in the room was completely silent and focused on them.

"You come right up to the front, dear," Mrs. Mallard said, grabbing her by the arm and taking her to the centre *barre*. She had her stand her in front of Anna and Grace and across from Alexandra and Tristan. Kaitlyn gulped.

"Now class, Kaitlyn's already done this work and taken her exam. She's done quite well, in fact." She squeezed Kaitlyn's arm fondly. "So, since the rest of you haven't learned the Advanced II syllabus yet, I'll have Kaitlyn demonstrate each exercise once, and then the rest of you will give it a go. Any questions? No? All right then, why don't we begin. *Pliés* please, Kaitlyn dear."

The rest of the class watched with disgust as Kaitlyn performed the *pliés*. RAD required highly exaggerated artistry in the higher levels, but halfway through the exercise Kaitlyn turned her head to do a *port de bras* and caught a glimpse of the others' expressions, which ranged from amusement to utter disgust (the last one belonging to Anna). She immediately blanked out her face, closed her mouth tightly, and managed to finish the exercise without making a choreographic mistake. As the last notes from the piano died away, Taylor held up her hand to stifle her laugh.

"Well, that was just lovely, wasn't it?" Mrs. Mallard demanded of the class. "Kaitlyn, that was technically gorgeous, and I loved your grasp of the artistry of the exercise in the beginning. But halfway through, you lost it a bit. I want you to work on keeping that emotional involvement all the way through. Don't get too focused on the technical aspects of the exercise." Kaitlyn nodded, keeping her eyes down.

"All right, now why don't all of you give it a try? Kaitlyn, dear, do it again will you, so they have someone to copy? Thank you, dear."

After they finished the *barre* exercises, Mrs. Mallard turned to Tristan, Kageki, and Jonathon, and, with a small angry nod, said, "Well, I see you haven't remembered a thing I tried to teach you last year. You obviously don't learn anything correctly in your other classes, and you don't seem to care. If you don't want a career, by all means, ignore me. You can leave and just take Mr. Yu's class. I'm sure he'll get you prepared to join a company. You know, Tristan," she walked over to him and gave him a tight smile. "You were actually improving last year. I had hopes that you were actually maturing. Evidently not.

"You know Andrew Lu," she said, putting her finger on her chin and reminiscing. "Now Andrew Lu, he always paid such attention to detail. I remember he would even take extra RAD classes that weren't even his level, just so he could *make sure* he had the basics completely down, especially when he was preparing for the Solo Seal. And you know, he got his Solo Seal Award. All that hard work, it paid off. Now he's dancing with the Royal Ballet in England. And mark my words, it's not the tricks and the show off steps that got him there, it's that clean training, that attention to detail."

George snorted from behind the piano. "I remember when Andy was here. He always came late, and you were always yelling at him for practising his *pirouettes* when he was supposed to be working on some *adage* exercise or something."

"George!" Mrs. Mallard interrupted. "I am trying to provide them with a positive role model! There are enough negative role models in this school without adding Andrew into the mix. And he did receive his Solo Seal, anyway. Let's continue."

After they'd finished the second *adage*, she walked up to Alexandra. The rest of the class anxiously moved out of her sightlines. "Alexandra, I am absolutely fed up." Alexandra swallowed hard and leaned back as far as she could. "Every year I tell you, you have potential. But if you are going to persist in slopping about and doing everything your own way, then I simply cannot help you. Every time, every time, I tell you that your legs are simply too high. Your hips are all over the place. You have no control, and it's just ugly. That's all there is to it. Now, just look at Grace, or Keiko. They both keep their legs far lower than you, but it's clean! And that's what matters, Alexandra. Not height."

Alexandra stood, chin firmly up and lips pressed tightly together. Mrs. Mallard went on, as if they could read her mind, "And you know what? That is why you got bronze." Alexandra looked up, hopeful that Mrs. Mallard might actually say something nice. "Yes. You need technique, good, solid technique and placement to get gold. With only tricks and high extensions, bronze is all you'll get. Leonie had clean technique, that's why she got gold. Alexandra, you just have to use your brain and dance with more physicality."

Mrs. Mallard finally turned around, and Alexandra glared at her back with as much venom as she could muster. "All right, let's move on to centre practice. Kaitlyn, dear, please show the class the first *port de bras*?"

As usual, Mrs. Mallard let them out 15 minutes late. They all skidded into the rehearsal room. Mr. Demidovski was at the front of the room giving a speech, but he paused as they came in to stare at them. "So glad you could join us," Mr. Moretti, who was standing next to Mr. Demidovski, said sarcastically. Mr. Demidovski's face creased in annoyance.

"Sorry, Mrs. Mallard kept us late. RAD class," Tristan explained.

"Next time, don't be late," Mr. Demidovski said. "The rehearsal, the preparation, it is very important." He gestured his arms towards them all grandly and said, "The

Vancouver International Ballet Academy ... we are all friends. We all love each other. We are all a happy family."

At this Kageki put his arm around Tristan. "My brother!"

Tristan laughed and put his arm around Julian. "Yeah, we all heart each other."

Julian pulled away from Tristan and grabbed his water bottle.

"Yes, we all love each other," Mr. Demidovski continued. "Mr. Demidovski, Mrs. Demidovski, we both give you the love, the passion. That is why we rent the Vancouver Centre for you, to give you the chance to perform on this world-class stage. We spend much money to give you this chance, this opportunity.

"In return, we expect, we want, you to give us your heart. You must do your best, eh? Mr. Demidovski give you 100 percent, you must give me 210 percent! It must be this way. Many people come to this performance, many rich people, many ballet people. Mr. Demidovski wants to give them a good show, eh? If no good feet, nice line, Mr. Demidovski is embarrassed. You must be thin, long line. There's only a week until the show, must be perfect. Mr. Demidovski give you the beautiful costumes, you must make them look good. Take care of the physical, eh? Lots of vegetable, some yogurt. No sugar, no cake ... after the show Mr. Demidovski doesn't care what you do, but before the show you must take care. Also the technique, must work in the class. Apple must look like apple, orange must look like orange, no look like potato, no look like ..." Mr. Demidovski paused, momentarily at loss for words. "… melon. When the ballet people come, they must have a good show! They must want to see you dance more. In the intermission, we do not want the audience to go get wine, we want them to stay, talk, wonder what will happen next. You must be good so they forget about the wine!"

"Is he saying that we will be responsible for turning the audience into alcoholics if we are hideous?" Alexandra whispered to Grace.

"Yep, pretty much. The sight of fat is proven to turn people into raging alcoholics!"

"So … anorexics are the same as AA?"

Kaitlyn giggled before she could stop herself. She didn't want them to know that she'd been listening. Grace and Alexandra immediately bent their heads together and whispered something inaudible, then giggled loudly. Kaitlyn blushed; they were obviously talking about her.

"Mr. Demidovski wants to be proud when he shows everyone his academy. If the show is no good, they will say that the academy is no good, and Mr. Demidovski will be ashamed. I will dig myself a grave." Mr. Demidovski looked around at them to make sure that they understood the gravity of this statement. "Mr. Demidovski will dig himself a grave because he is so ashamed.

"Must work!" he said in a vague attempt to summarize his speech. "Anyone else have anything to say?" he asked the other teachers. "Questions?" he asked the students.

"'Trepak' will rehearse first, and then 'Mirliton,'" Mr. Moretti announced. "The rest of you may go." Kaitlyn got up, glad not to be rehearsing for once. She walked into the hall and sat down to pull off her *pointe* shoes.

"I just don't know what to do after dinner," one of the younger students was complaining nearby. "Like, I'm fine all day, and then wham, I start eating. I'm trying not to eat anything after five o'clock, but then I keep going to get stuff."

"Like what?" one of the other girls asked.

"Well, we have this fruit bowl in the living room…." There was a collective groan of understanding.

"Did you know that a banana has just as many carbs as a cup of rice?"

"What? You're kidding, right? Great. It's just so hard to stay up and study without something to munch on."

"What I do is, I make some ice. And then I break it up, so it's all in little chips. It actually works. You're munching on something, but there aren't any calories."

"That's an awesome idea! I need something to occupy me. Days off are the worst, all I seem to do is eat."

"Do you know what's great for days off? A lettuce smoothie. You can throw in ice and celery too, but make it mostly lettuce. It's great, it really fills you up."

"Uh, no offence, but that sounds kinda gross."

"Actually, I think I want to try it. Do you want to make one with me when you come over on Sunday?"

Kaitlyn got up and left. She wondered if the whole ice chips thing would actually work. It was worth a try, anyway. She wrapped her hands around her waist as she walked downstairs, trying to feel how far apart her fingertips were from joining in the back.

Downstairs, Jessica was taking orders for the next Yumiko shipment. Kaitlyn knelt down to gaze at the brochure. The sample fabrics were so pretty. Taylor was sitting cross-legged, hogging the signup sheet and the brochures. "I like the Alex one," she was telling Keiko. "I'm not sure about the colours, yet, though."

"Wow, how many bodysuits are you ordering?" Kaitlyn asked as she looked at the paper with everyone's orders on it.

"Um ... five so far," Taylor said, giggling. "My mom said no more than five, but they are so pretty!"

"They do look gorgeous," Angela said with a sigh. "But I really can't afford any right now." Everyone except Jessica ignored her.

"Aren't your parents kind of rich?" Jessica asked.

"Well, sort of, But they don't approve of spending money on bodysuits when we can only wear them for rehearsals."

Kaitlyn looked wistfully at the colours. She was pretty sure that her mom was going to get her one for Christmas, but she really wished she had it to wear right now. The colours were so bright and rich compared to the academy uniforms.

She wandered off to get changed, choosing not to torture herself over bodysuits she'd have to wait for. She went to the mirror and began undoing her bun, the long coil making one big curl as she took out the pins. She debated whether to risk taking the ponytail out or not. She was getting a serious headache. She pulled out the elastics, but her hair stayed in position thanks to the gel.

Kaitlyn sighed and wetted her brush, starting to attack her hair in an attempt to make it look normal.

"I hate hair bumps," Chloe said, stacking her stuff on the other side of the sink.

Kaitlyn winced at her voice. She couldn't handle bright, happy people at the moment, especially ones that were half her size.

"Geez, stop taking up the entire counter!" Anna said in an annoyed tone as she came up behind them.

"Oh, sorry!" Chloe blushed as she moved her things over.

"Oh, that's okay, I didn't know it was *your* stuff. You can keep it there if you want."

Kaitlyn's stomach clenched, and she hurried to gather up her stuff. As she left the changing room, she paused to look at a photograph of Leonie Camden. *My arabesque is way higher,* Kaitlyn thought, pain flitting across her features. *But Leonie is skinnier and so pretty with that soft little face.* She shook her head violently in an attempt to clear it. She quickly looked around to see if anybody had been watching her. Relieved, she saw only general program parents and their kids. Before she made it to the door, a little girl came up to her and showed off her runs on demi-*pointe*.

"I'm a ballet dancer," the little girl said excitedly. "That's why I can go on my tippy-toes. See?"

"Er, yes I see," Kaitlyn said. "Um … good job."

The girl's mother took this as genuine interest in her obviously prodigiously gifted child. She shoved the child closer to Kaitlyn, saying "She can already do skips, too!

She's only four, but she has such natural talent for the ballet. Her teacher says she has very good feet, very rare."

"Um, yes ..." Kaitlyn said, trying to leave.

"Look, I can go all the way up!" The girl rose to the tops of her toes and promptly crumpled down again.

Julian, who had come out of rehearsal to fill up his water bottle, grinned. "Obviously she is going to be a great ballet dancer," he said to the mother, putting a serious expression on his face and winking at Kaitlyn.

The mother beamed at him. "Yes, a ballerina!"

"Seriously, though, don't *do* that," Kaitlyn said as the girl rose to her toes and crumpled again. This time, one of her ankles twisted into the floor on the way down. "You are really going to hurt yourself." The mother glared at her.

Kaitlyn's parents were both in the car when she got outside. "Where are we going?" Kaitlyn asked.

"To your grandparents' for dinner, I told you this morning," Cecilia said.

Kaitlyn deflated. She loved her grandparents, but all she really felt like doing was punching somebody, flying away on a plane somewhere, or, at the very least, becoming somebody else. She knew that the whole dinner would be spent discussing her fabulous ballet career and how it could be better achieved. "Can I maybe go home instead? I really don't feel well."

"What do you mean, you don't feel well?" Jeff asked. "You look fine to me."

"Don't be ridiculous, Kaitlyn," Cecilia said. Kaitlyn sunk down into her seat and started to cry. "What's *wrong* with you?!" Cecilia turned around in her seat.

"Stop. Here's a Kleenex." Kaitlyn grabbed one and blew her nose, then just grabbed the whole box.

"Did something happen?" Jeff asked.

"No! Just go away!" Kaitlyn wailed. She began to sob hysterically. Her mother told her to stop it and just grow up, as Jeff pulled the car out of the lot.

Chapter Ten

Taylor Audley
hahaha Keiko burnnnnnnnnnn :D Love you, hate you,
woodn't wont to date you jkjkjkjk bahha fattttteeee So
nervous :S for rehearsal :D blarg :S

Taylor's alarm clock roused her from a marvellous
dream. She jerked herself violently off the bed. "*F*!
Ouch!" She swore again, accidentally tripping over the
textbooks that lay on the floor beside her bed. She had
meant to study when she went to bed, hence her laptop
and textbooks all over the floor — and the blue ball-
point pen that had exploded all over her sheets, she
just noticed ... "Shi-shitake mushrooms!" *Really,* she
thought, *I might as well just go back to bed.* Today wasn't
looking terribly promising.

She had meant to do her homework last night, but
had been side-tracked by a thread on the *Ballet Talk*
forum that had mentioned Alexandra. It was seriously
vicious. *I wonder if she's seen it?* Taylor thought, secretly
hoping that she had. She kicked her right leg with her
left one. "Don't be a bitch," she said out loud.

She reached out her arms directly in front and then
swung them around to the back. She heard her back
crack satisfyingly. She then toppled her upper body
down toward her feet, feeling her hamstrings wince from

yesterday's work. She swung her head and crossed arms around, bumping her elbows on the ground. Her body was starting to loosen up. Finally, she swung her head to touch her feet, pressed her body to her legs, then she swung up and cracked both hips. *Oh, head rush much!*

Alison barged in, demanding to know what Taylor had done with her book report book.

"I don't know!" Taylor was indignant. "I'm dyslexic. Do I *look* like I go around reading other people's books?"

Alison ignored her. Her book was on top of the pile of textbooks on the floor. "I can see that you got a lot of homework done last night," she said sarcastically. "These are my books!"

"What? Well ... how come you didn't notice if you did *your* homework?"

"I'd already done it," Alison answered smugly. Taylor rolled her eyes, unable to think of a comeback.

"Go away! Your homework is baby stuff, it should take you like five minutes to finish it!"

Taylor went down to the kitchen in a foul mood. "Do you want some toast, Tay-honey?" Charlize asked with false cheerfulness.

Taylor muttered, "No thanks," and poured herself a glass of chocolate milk.

"Taylor, why don't you have something healthy with that?"

"This is healthy!" Taylor protested. "It has calcium, and other stuff. Milk is healthy."

Alison rolled her eyes. "It's not when it's got that much sugar in it."

"Ali's right, Taylor."

"Okay, fine!" Taylor set the half-full glass down on the table. "I won't drink it if it bothers you that much."

"Taylor, you have to have something for breakfast." Taylor shrugged and went to get her stuff.

For once, she managed to catch the early bus. *I might actually get that homework done,* she thought hopefully. She fished out her iPod and tried to listen to it, but she was too jittery. She unplugged her earphones and began tapping her fingers and feet, staring out the window. She felt the bus moving, making her stomach tense.

As they went over the bridge, Taylor imagined the bus speeding up, faster and faster …. and then *boom! Pow!* She pictured the explosion in her head, seeing the bus crumple, everyone instantly dead…. Taylor immediately felt guilty. She didn't really want the other passengers to die. But somehow, she really didn't care if she did or not. Which was pretty weird now that she thought about it, since she cared so much about what she did with her life and was scared of so many things. *I don't think I'd be particularly upset if I found out that I was going to die in a moment,* Taylor decided. *Only if there was going to be pain.* She bit her lip, wondering if there was anyone up there listening to her. "Sorry, God," she mouthed silently, just in case.

She reached into her bag and pulled out one of her new *pointe* shoes, a needle threaded with floss, and a ribbon already cut and burnt, and began to sew the ribbon onto the shoe. She started to feel a bit calmer and sewed happily.

By the time Taylor got to McKinley, both of her shoes were sewn. She ran to the school bathroom to fix her hair. The rain always made it go all wavy, a look she didn't particularly like. While she was putting on her lip gloss, she suddenly remembered that she had to do her homework. But, once she got to the study hall and reached into her bag for her books, she stopped breathing. She'd brought her day one books and work instead of her day two work. She looked up and down the study hall. She couldn't see anyone from the academy or any of her teachers for the day. She flew down the stairs and out the door before she met anyone she knew.

Taylor went to the bus stop she knew that nobody from the academy used. It was raining fairly heavily now, and she had forgotten her umbrella, again. She was at the comfortable stage of wetness, where you're already soaked so it doesn't really matter that it's raining. In fact, the rain falling seemed warmer than the water soaking Taylor's clothes, so it was sort of pleasant. She did a travelling *pas de bourée* and a *pirouette en dedans*. She came to an abrupt stop when she saw that Julian was already at the bus stop. She stood still, desperately searching her brain for an excuse that would fit.

"Hey," said Julian. "What are you doing here? Skipping?"

It suddenly occurred to Taylor that Julian had no business at that bus stop either. "Um, what are you doing?"

"Skipping. Don't tell Tristan and Kageki, though. They are such uber-keeners. I totally needed a day off. I'm going crazy."

"Oh," Taylor said defensively. "Well, I'm skipping,

too. But because I got mixed up on which day it was, so I brought the wrong textbooks and stuff, so I didn't have my homework, and I didn't do it last night, anyway. Today totally sucks, so I'm going to skip."

"Why don't you just tell your teachers that you got mixed up with the days? They're really nice about it, I've done it before. I mean, they look at you like you're an idiot, but that's survivable."

"I can't," said Taylor, jutting her lip out and making a hole in the gravel around the bus-stop pole with her toe. "I miss my homework too much. And I'm, like, failing math and English and science ..."

"But for math aren't you in—" Julian stopped himself, embarrassed, realizing what he had been about to say. He wiped away the water trickling down his face.

"Loser math? Yes. *And* I have a whole block of skills development, and ... I don't know. I take Ritalin and stuff, but it doesn't seem to help. And I never seem to have any time for my homework because of dance and stuff." Taylor frowned.

Julian had slipped his backpack off and was digging his lunch out.

"Julian ... Jules, It's only like 7:45-ish! And if you open up your lunch right now, the rain will get in and ruin it."

"I'm hungry, so whatever!" When he opened his container, rain immediately began splashing in. Taylor started laughing, watching him try to eat the wet white rice with the rain doing its best to wash it off the fork. "Want a chicken foot?" Julian grinned as he pointed it out with his fork.

"Ew, no! Gross. Mrs. Yu is the weirdest cook. You look so funny." She watched him eat it. "Really, you look like you should be the stupid one."

"Who says I get honour roll?" asked Julian, wiping fried egg off his mouth. "I'm not like Tristan and the rest either, I'm a strictly C student. B if I'm lucky. But seriously," Julian said between mouthfuls, "are we the only mediocre students from the academy? Because that totally sucks if it's true."

"Basically, yes," Taylor sighed. "At least of the ones who are good at dance. Like, Alexandra gets straight As ..."

"Tristan, too," Julian said, rolling his eyes.

"Nobody knows about Kaitlyn, yet, though."

"Oh yeah, right. She's new too." Julian quickly stuffed his lunch in his backpack as the bus approached.

They got on and sat down on one of the benches, Taylor getting the window seat.

"Where are you going before rehearsal?" Taylor asked, suddenly shy. She hadn't really talked to Julian before. The people he hung out with most at the academy terrified her.

"Um ... rehearsal ..." said Julian, suddenly looking nervous. "Okay, I, like, *really* don't want to go to that."

"Don't you want to be a dancer?"

"Well yes, of course. I mean, I *think* so. But we haven't had a day off since October."

"We never do."

"Well, I want to have one, and I pick today. Do you think Mr. Moretti would kick me out if I skipped?"

"No. You're a boy. A tall one. He needs you." Julian looked relieved. "But say that you're sick. That way they can pretend they believe you, and it'll just work better."

"Hey, do you want to come with me?" Julian asked suddenly.

"Where are you going?"

"No idea!"

"I'd love to. But I'll be kicked out. I'm not a boy, and I've only got *corps* roles."

"Come on," Julian wheedled.

"All right," Taylor said, taking a deep breath. "I will."

They both phoned, one after another, and made Gabriel promise to remember to tell Mr. Moretti.

"Now where are we going?" Julian asked.

"I don't know. But we better decide soon. I don't want to waste our day off on the bus."

"For sure! I know, let's go to Whole Foods and get some food first."

"You *just* ate!"

"Yeah, but I didn't like it. And I'm growing! I *need* food."

"Growing, sure, but which direction?"

"Hey! For your information, I'm as skinny as a rail. Even Mr. Yu said I needed to eat more meat so I would have 'good muscles like Leon.' And I'm even skinnier than Tristan."

"For how much longer?" Taylor asked, laughing. "Okay, we'll go to Whole Foods."

Julian rang the bell just in time, and they got off the bus. "Want to wait for the other bus or just walk?" he asked, shrugging his shoulders into his backpack.

"Let's just walk. It'll be warmer that way." They walked the rest of the way in silence; the noise of the rain and the wet that was becoming uncomfortably cold were conversation deterrents. Finally they got to Whole Foods. Julian plunked his backpack on one of the benches.

"Islander! It might not be safe leaving our bags," snorted Taylor, but she put hers down, too.

"Hey, I lived in Toronto, too!"

"It didn't seem to take," Taylor teased. Julian grinned.

They started at the produce section and worked their way across the store to the prepared food, arguing over every section. Taylor thought that the sole purpose of food was to give you a sugar high, while Julian believed that food was a statement about what kind of a person you were.

"Organic food is not a waste of time and money! Like, seriously, do you want a million chemicals in your body, not to mention the ground? Why do you think we have cancer and obesity nowadays?"

"Soy milk is *so* gross! Omigod, I didn't know they even had almond milk. Hemp milk? You have *got* to be kidding me."

"Okay, but have you even *tried* goji berries?"

"Brown sugar is healthy, you know. It's only the white kind that isn't."

"Okay, I'm going to buy a carton of soy ice cream to split, and you can see if you like it the same as dairy ice cream."

"Hippy."

When they got back to their table, Julian picked up his backpack with a grin. "Islander wins!"

"You got lucky," Taylor said. She picked up her bag to check that her *pointe* shoes were still there.

Julian started dividing up their food. Taylor frowned. She picked up one of the napkins and started shredding it into little pieces, kicking the table leg.

"Are you okay?"

"Do you think Mr. Moretti will kick me out?"

"I dunno. But he can't really kick you out of everything, can he? I mean, it is a school, not a company. You're paying them, they aren't paying you."

"True." Taylor's eyes welled up. "But it's Mr. Moretti."

"Yeah," Julian said, uncomfortable. "Um, do you want some ice cream?"

Taylor took the proffered bowl with both hands. She tried it warily. "Hey, I like it!"

"Told you! Eat some more," he urged her as he finished his muffin and moved onto his salad. "I'm going to eat it all if you don't take it."

"That's okay." Taylor took a spoonful of her ice cream and smooshed it against the bowl until it melted. "I'm not that hungry." She looked up and watched Julian eat for a while. "You are so going to puke."

"What? No, I won't," Julian assured her as he moved onto the ice cream.

"You're getting better in *pas* class, hey?" Taylor said casually.

Julian looked up, surprised. "I hope so. I mean, that's the idea, isn't it?"

Taylor laughed, a bit too heartily. "Yeah."

"What was wrong with me before? I wasn't that bad, was I?"

"No ..." Taylor answered slowly. "And you're tall, so that's good. Do you know yet if the Demidovskis want you to do a *pas* in festival?"

Julian shrugged, not looking up. "Not likely, is it? I mean, I didn't get a *pas* in *The Nutcracker*."

Taylor fidgeted nervously. "Well, you could just ask to do one."

"Yeah. But who's gonna want to do it with me? Lexi? Yeah, right."

"I would do one with you."

Julian looked up, surprised. "Oh. Cool. Yeah, that'd be fun."

Taylor nodded and bit the head off the dark chocolate Santa she'd been saving.

"Oh, sweetie! That is amazing," Charlize said, gasping into the phone. "I can't believe it! That is the best thing that's happened to you all year."

"I know," Taylor said, smiling as she snuggled into the bus seat with her cellphone clutched to her ear, thankful for the heater vent next to her feet. She felt a warm glow of satisfaction spread through her as she answered her mother's many questions. She, Taylor Audley, was going to do a *pas de deux* with Julian Reese, the boy with more potential than anybody since Andrew Lu. Perhaps including Andrew Lu. He hadn't been tall, despite his talent.

Chapter Eleven

Alexandra Dunstan
"Take me I'm alive, never was a girl with a wicked mind, but everything looks better, when the sun goes down..."

It was still mostly dark when Justin dropped Alexandra off at McKinley, and the early morning air was cold. Alexandra shivered as she went up the steps, her feet and hands freezing. She shook her limbs, trying to get some circulation back into her hands and feet. Inside, Grace was already sitting at a table. Alexandra went to join her. "Nobody else here yet?"

"Tristan," Grace said, staring blindly at her socials book. "He's in the washroom putting gel in his hair."

Alexandra dug out her textbook and tried to finish her homework.

"Can I copy yours?" Grace asked. Alexandra pressed her lips together hard. She really hated it when Grace copied her homework. "Please." Grace's plea sounded more like a command.

Alexandra passed Grace her notebook, forcing them to sit closer together. "There you go, nice to be nice," Grace said as she began to copy. "Your writing is so messy I can hardly read it."

"Good," Alexandra said under her breath. Then she

said out loud, "That's what happens when you do home-work at one in the morning."

As Alexandra worked and Grace copied, Grace told her how Mr. Demidovski had asked Leon to work with her on the *Black Swan pas* for a special charity perfor-mance, and how she was *so* busy this year she just didn't know how she was going to fit it all in, she certainly wasn't going to be able fit in festival, too. Alexandra rolled her eyes: the real reason Grace wouldn't be doing festival was that she never did well, while Alexandra always did. She didn't mention that Mrs. Demidovski had asked her to do a *pas* with Tristan.

Alexandra waited for the bus after school in a foul mood. She tried not to listen as Taylor go on and on about how she hoped Mr. Moretti wouldn't be "like, mad at me!" because she was sick yesterday. Alexandra imagined punching Taylor in the face. The bus was late, and Alexandra's feet and hands were numb by the time she got on. She sat down on one of the middle benches, avoiding the noise everyone else was making in the back. Tristan came and sat down next to her.

"Look," Tristan said, pointing out the window. Kaitlyn was running for the bus, but it pulled away and she was left behind. Tristan and Alexandra both laughed.

"Sometimes life just works out," she said.

"Definitely. What's in that?" he asked as Alexandra pulled out a thermos.

"Chocolate protein powder, hot water, and this Echinacea anti-cold mix." She opened it carefully, trying not to spill any of the contents on herself. "Where are your sidekicks today?" Julian and Kageki were not on the bus.

"They both had to see their counsellors. Kageki wants to transfer out of ESL English to normal English because he's doing fine in all his other courses, and Julian wants to transfer out of French because he's failing it."

"Seriously?"

"Yup. He's going to take it online this summer, instead."

"And he's going to do this when? If he can't pass it with the whole school year and a teacher, how does he expect to pass it online, without a teacher, in only a couple of weeks, during summer school?"

"I don't think he knows about summer intensives," Tristan said, laughing. "I asked where he went last year and he said 'mostly the beach.'"

They were interrupted by Anna, who'd come to sit on the bench in front of them. "Hey, Trissie. I was looking for you. Mrs. Demidovski asked me the other day if I'd like to do a *pas de deux* with you this year in festival." At this, Alexandra accidentally spilled some of her drink on herself. "But I'm going with my family to Hawaii during festival."

"What? The Demidovskis are letting you do that right before the June show?" Alexandra exclaimed in spite of herself.

"Sure. Why wouldn't they?" Alexandra glared at her and shrugged, sitting back in her seat again, sulking as she drank her mixture. Anna went back to sit with Grace, and they burst out laughing.

"Do you have any gum?" Tristan asked after searching through his pockets.

"No. You should just smoke," she teased. "You know what Mr. Yu says, the more you smoke, the higher you jump."

Tristan snorted. "Yeah. I can see how great it's made Dmitri jump."

"You know, you're probably the only one of the older boys who doesn't smoke. Except Julian. Does he smoke?"

"It's not a question of *does* he smoke, as of *what* he smokes," Tristan said, giggling. "He is such a little granola-muncher."

Alexandra laughed. "I should have known. I was walking down the hallway at the academy the other day, and he looked shocked when he saw me. And then he started looking around like he was seeing little fairies everywhere. I thought he'd just taken too much cold medication or something. "

"Nope! People don't get that laid back naturally."

"He's probably ingested enough from the air on the Island to be naturally like that! At least now I know what to get him for Secret Santa!"

"True," Tristan said, laughing. "That is so weird that you two got each other for Secret Santa!"

At that moment the clamour from the back suddenly increased, and they both turned to see what was happening. Two of the younger girls were trying to feed one of the little boys some of Taylor's hard candies.

They'd told told him that they were birth control pills.

"No, no!" he yelled. "Birth control makes you gay!"

"I thought that was soy milk," Alexandra said. "And all the time it was birth control."

"Well, *that* explains a lot," said Tristan, shaking his head sadly. "Remind me to cut back on my birth control use." They both laughed quietly as they turned back to their lunches. "So, I guess I get out of a *pas de deux* this year." Tristan's voice was full of false cheer. "That's great. I mean, now I have more time to work on my solos."

"Um, yeah, about that. Mrs. Demidovski asked me yesterday if I wanted to do a *pas de deux* with you. I guess I'm second choice. I can say no if you really don't want to do it."

"No, that's great!" Tristan quickly assured her. "Did she mention if they had decided which one?"

"Nope," Alexandra said, taking Tristan's bag of carrots from him. "Any one that you want?"

"Ah … *Sleeping Beauty* or *Black Swan*?"

"I'd love *Black Swan*, but I don't know if they'll let us. Otherwise, sure, *Sleeping Beauty* … I'd like *Le Corsaire* or *Blue Bird* too, but since we're both doing *Sleeping Beauty* variations, it'd be kinda nice to have it all themed. Who's Julian doing a *pas* with?" Alexandra asked curiously.

"No idea," Tristan said, passing her his apple.

"Thanks," said Alexandra. "Puffed corn?" He took a handful.

"I don't think he's doing festival," Tristan continued. "He said the Demidovskis haven't talked to him about it, and he won't do anything on his own steam."

"Mr. Yu will make him. He wouldn't let a boy from his homestay do nothing."

"Yes, we wouldn't want to besmirch the family honour," Tristan snickered.

Mr. Yu was downstairs trying to shift some of the backdrop and props to find something

"Mr. Yu!" Cromwell Gilly said as he ran down the stairs in a panic. "Where did you put the flowers for the 'Trepak' head pieces?" Mr. Yu began arguing with Cromwell Gilly, saying that he should have moved them out of the storage room before he started moving the sets around, and Cromwell Gilly started arguing that Mr. Yu needed to move "that stupid Christmas tree off of my costumes now!" He looked like he was close to tears and/or slapping Mr. Yu.

Alexandra shook her head as she witnessed the scene and went to her locker to change for classes. She pulled out her bodysuit and looked at it for a second. It was completely faded and was stretched out of shape, making it extremely unflattering. It looked a couple of years old instead of just the couple of months that it was. Alexandra made a decision. Since they hadn't cast her well, and they never helped her, she wouldn't wear their stupid uniform. It wasn't like the boys ever did. *And besides, what can they do to me? Yell at me? Not cast me? Give other people solos and* pas de deux *ahead of me?* The corner of her mouth turned up a little in a smile at the thought of her rebellion. She put the uniform back in her locker and looked through the rest of her bodysuits. Not red or pink, she wasn't going to push it that far. *There, perfect!* She pulled out an old favourite: a beautiful blue bodysuit that was the kind of fabric that never seemed to fade. She went into the bathroom and changed into it. She did her hair, admiring the way her striped warm-ups went with the colour of the bodysuit.

Grace came into the bathroom just then and said, "Do you have a private or something?"

"Nope!" Alexandra blushed and added a quickly made-up excuse. "My uniform bodysuit is still damp." She added a sparkly pin to her bun, something she hadn't bothered to do in a while.

Grace raised her eyebrows. "Okay, but you'd better make sure the Demidovskis don't see you." She set down her stuff and began to do her hair. Alexandra finished her hair and added some more makeup, carefully applying sparkly silver eyeliner to her top lid and more black eyeliner on the bottom.

"You're wearing a lot of makeup today, Lexi," Grace said. Alexandra shrugged, not bothering to answer, and finished with her eyeliner. She turned around to view her profile and tugged her bodysuit down a bit in the front. *You can get away with pulling your bodysuit down pretty low if you don't have boobs,* she thought, chuckling to herself.

She went upstairs and sat down next to Tristan, Julian, and Kageki, starting to stretch. Kageki was playing a game on his PSP, with his own sound effects.

"Boys are so weird," she said and got up and stood next to the wall, using it to prop herself up as she pulled her leg past her head. Then she went and lay down next to Tristan, stretching her turn-out. They listened in on Chloe's father and Michael's mother talking as they waited in the hallway. They were sitting in chairs in the middle of the hallway watching classes, as usual.

"Well, Kate and I think it is very important to stress that academics are important, too. We always tell Chloe that she has to do well at school."

"Yeah, I believe that, too. But I always tell Tony that we have to understand that Michael has a gift, and we have to make allowances so that he is able to develop that gift."

David Song interrupted her quickly. "I do understand that. We realize that Chloe is very special, but we set our children up to succeed. We want it to be *possible* for Chloe to succeed in both academics and dance. And she does, she certainly does." He sat back proudly, confident of having proven his point.

Tristan rolled his eyes at Alexandra. She shook her head, smothering her giggles with her hand. Tristan rolled over onto his back and prepared to go up into a bridge.

"I don't think my parents set me up to succeed," Alexandra whispered to him as he started to push up. "I feel cheated." Tristan collapsed, unable to complete the bridge while laughing. Alexandra went up into a bridge while Tristan tried to stop laughing. She slowly walked her hands to her ankles and managed to grab her left ankle with her left hand. She tried to do the same with her right hand, but lost her balance and fell over.

* * *

"How are you? How was class?" Beth asked during dinner.

"Good," Alexandra said. "It was fun."

"What was good about it?"

"I don't know, nothing particularly. It was just a good day. Oh, and I *am* doing a *pas de deux* with Tristan for festival. I just have to talk to Mrs. Demidovski about it and arrange privates."

"That's great. It's nice to see you coming out of there happy again."

"Mom!"

"What? It is." They spent the rest of dinner discussing various costume options for competition, since it was only the two of them for dinner. Everyone else was out.

Alexandra went up to her room after dinner, yawning. It had been a long day. *Thank goodness I didn't have rehearsal today,* Alexandra thought. *I* need *sleep.* Before she went to bed she checked her email and deleted what felt like a million Facebook requests. She told herself to go to bed, but couldn't help herself. She logged onto *Ballet Talk*; she hadn't checked it for a while. She scrolled down through the forum, not seeing anything of interest until she spotted a thread called "Genee Results" with posts that were only a couple of days old. She clicked on it excitedly, wondering if they had said anything about her. *Blah, blah,* she thought, skimming to the more recent posts. She felt a little glow of happiness as she saw the words "Bronze = Alexandra Dunstan, Canada (Vancouver International Ballet Academy)." She scrolled through other posts praising the gold winner — for control? Alexandra reread it in disbelief. *That girl had tremendous potential and talent, which was why she had gotten gold, but control? Hardly.* They mentioned silver briefly: a boy. He was good, had nice tricks, and a clean, not particularly interesting performance. Alexandra laughed at that; he'd been able to impersonate every judge and teacher they'd had during the competition with deadly accuracy. And finally herself!

First, just an acknowledgement that she won, and yes, she was Canadian. Then:

> Isn't Alexandra Dunstan the "North-American Somova?" I am thinking about a tall, hyper-extended, somewhat-vulgar teenager who butchered Petipa's choreography for Kitri at the YAGP finals last year? Tricks over substance and style. Sorry, but she totally made me think about Somova while watching her in the finals. Genee used to have higher standards … if I'm thinking about the same person.

"Ouch," Alexandra whispered to herself. *Vulgar?* Then there was a question about the gold winner and a post asking if it was really appropriate to call a sixteen-year old vulgar, and the original poster had responded:

Indeed, it is Sky Landon from
Britain. Her magnificence and
modesty simply highlighted
Dunstan's weaknesses. As to
"somewhat vulgar" — I stand by
the statement 100%. Competitors
expose themselves. If they can't
take the truth, they shouldn't be
there. Ditto the parents. Smug,
prolonged smiles at the audience
should be reserved for Liberty
Belle in the "Stars and Stripes"
pas or the four ballerinas in
Grand Pas de Quatre. Then again,
there are extraordinary "kids"
who take the risk at an early
age and merit the kudos, such as
Takuya Nakamura, also at Genee.
Extraordinary ability, yet modest.
No need to "milk" the crowd.

Alexandra stared at the computer in disbelief. She
began to cry. Genee had been so much fun, she had
thought that everyone had liked her ... had the audience really just sat there thinking she was embarrassing
herself? Why would they give her bronze then? She
blew her nose and continued reading.

I think it's quite right to call
her execution vulgar and if she
makes a professional career
that will soon change. What I
do not like, and I do realize
I am watching a film and it's
quite different to being at a
performance, is her feet. In
her attempt to dance fast she

hits poses without going on full
pointe **ugly, ugly ugly** and that
reminds me of certain Russian
dancers of the past who thought
that speed was what audiences
wanted, not finesse. Miss
Dunstan also irritates me by not
completing steps where the heels
should go fully down, before
going onto the next phrase. Even
at speed she should be doing
this. Watch Maximova in a series
of *pirouettes or fouettes*. Why
make a young girl emulate the
Sofiane Sylve video with the
multiple *pirouettes* when two
clean balanced *pirouettes* would
have had a more aesthetic and
competent looking effect. I have
hope for her, though.

And that was another poster! Apparently everyone
agreed. She sucked. Alexandra took a deep breath and
kept going. A few more posts saying that the post before
was too harsh and young dancers shouldn't be criticized
so severely, but nothing saying that they were wrong.
And another from the earlier poster:

As Mommy used to say "If you
can't take the heat, get out
of the kitchen." The dancers in
question are either pros or pre-
professional students presenting
themselves in competition, where
they should expect to be judged by
all who see them … not just the
panel of official judges. **They**

asked for it. Ballet Talkers know
about what they write and will
not be mere "Yes Men." Praise and
criticism come with the territory
of being a professional dancer
or an aspirant who presents
him/herself in competitions.
Hopefully, Ms. Dunstan's next year
of training will serve to **tame
her** because the raw talent was
definitely there. In fact, I'd
love to hear about her progress in
Vancouver, if anyone has seen her
of late (not just on YouTube).

So that's that. That's what everyone thought when they see me — vulgar. Alexandra pushed away from her computer and threw herself on her bed, sobbing. *Mr. Moretti is right, Mrs. Mallard is right, I'm terrible!* She stayed there crying until she felt like she had no tears left. She got up and blew her nose, undressed, turned off the light, and crawled into bed. She lay still, feeling her body push the mattress down. She pictured herself disappearing into the mattress more and more, just disappearing.... She could picture a really cool contemporary dance with that theme.

Chapter Twelve

Julian Reese
Show Time! Good luck everyone!

It was the day before *The Nutcracker*. After the rehearsal that morning, they'd been sent home for a rest. They were expected to be at the theatre at 9:00 a.m. the next morning. They probably wouldn't get out of there again until at least 10:00 p.m., later for the boys because Mr. Yu always made them help move the sets out of the theatre. Julian had taken the invitation to rest to heart, and had gone from the studio straight to bed. But now Leon was sitting on his bed, slapping his face.

"I'm up! I'm up!" Julian sprang up, angrily. "What are you doing in my room?"

"You have an I.D. now, right?"

"Sort of, I borrowed it. You're legal. What do you want my I.D. for?"

"I don't want your I.D. I just wanted to know if you have one. Let me see." Leon picked it up and looked at the picture. He started laughing. "I cannot believe that you managed to find someone with hair like you! What is up with this name? Caspian Ocean?"

"Everyone calls him Cas. I'm supposed to give it back when I go home the day after tomorrow."

"This is a real person?"

"Yeah…? I've known him since before I was born. His mom and my mom were friends while my mom was preggers with me, and his mom was preggers with his little sister."

"What's his sister called?"

Julian rolled his eyes. "Lyric Ocean. She's really pretty."

"I bet," Leon said, staring at the I.D. "Anyway, we wanted to know if you wanted to come with us? A bunch of us are going downtown to Number 5 to celebrate."

"Celebrate what?"

"*Nutcracker*'s tomorrow, isn't it?"

Julian shrugged. "Sure. Just let me get ready."

"Take your time. Mr. Yu's downtown arguing over the price of Duan's buns for dinner tomorrow."

When Mr. Yu got back, he was in a good mood. He'd managed to haggle the buns to five cents less than the year before, and he even got some custard tarts added for free. Julian, Mr. Yu, and Leon piled into the van, and Mr. Yu took off with a screech of protest from the elderly vehicle. He stopped at Broadway to pick up Dmitri, Jonathon, and a man Julian didn't recognize.

Inside, Leon hit Julian over the head. "Stop grinning, *Caspian*." Mr. Yu led them to the table and Dmitri hopped off to go get drinks.

"You have no idea how long it's been since I've gotten drunk," Julian said, sitting between Jonathon and Leon. "Nobody at the academy ever seems to do anything fun, and I haven't really had time to make friends at McKinley."

Dmitri came back with a pitcher of beer, and Julian poured himself a glass and downed half of it. "Like, it's an uber-preppy school," Julian explained. "If I wanted somebody to come over and help me with my math or … I dunno, start a band with violinists and pianists and like flautists, I'd be set. But going out drinking? That's when you'd have a hard time getting people to come. Unless you tried to pass it off as an anime party!" He finished the glass and poured himself another. "The beer kinda sucks, hey?"

"Yup," Leon said, laughing. "I'd take it easy there."

Julian shrugged, but he set his glass down for a second and Dmitri quickly refilled it. He looked over at the stripper on the stage. "I like her hair," he informed Leon before he finished his second glass.

"You buy the next," Mr. Yu barked across the table before turning back to his conversation with the man Julian didn't recognize (who was called Kang, apparently) and Dmitri. They were arguing about something. Suddenly Mr. Yu pulled out a pack of cards and called Jonathon over. Jonathon went over happily, smirking at Leon as he passed by.

Leon rolled his eyes but pulled the pitcher closer to himself and Julian. "They get the cards, we get the beer, fair's fair," he muttered. Julian raised his eyebrows as a question. "Majong," Leon explained, pouring them both another glass. "They need four."

Leon got up and went to get another pitcher, leaving Julian by himself. The others were absorbed in their game.

Julian sipped the rest of his beer, staring at the strippers. He noticed a tall brunette doing a backbend and started sniggering. Tristan could do that back bend so much better. The image of Tristan up there in those outfits flashed in his head. He finished his glass with a laugh.

When Leon came back with the pitcher, he asked what was so funny.. "Just … one of the strippers wasn't very flexible, and then I started thinking of people at the academy who were, and I got this mental image of Tristan up there," Julian explained, laughing as he poured himself a drink. "Thanks, man," he added, indicating the pitcher.

"No prob," Leon said. He poured himself another, took a sip, and put it down again with a grimace. "This stuff really is vile."

"Um … yeah," Julian said, feeling his stomach twist as he took another gulp. "I probably should have eaten something, but I couldn't find anything in the house except Wonder Bread, which I don't eat, and Cheerios. So I had a handful of dry Cheerios." He finished his glass and sat back, his hands on his stomach. He felt it lurch, and grimaced a little.

"Don't throw up on me!"

"It's okay," Julian reassured him. He poured himself another glass. He let his body slump, feeling the lovely warmth of beer all over his body. Leon's face disturbed his meditation. Julian took another gulp.

"Are you going to be okay for *Nutcracker* tomorrow?"

Julian thought about it. "Sure. See the stripper over there?" He pointed. "She looks like Delilah. But her hair is like my mom's."

Leon looked at him funny. "That's just disturbing," he said, shaking his head. "But you're right. She does look like Delilah."

Julian poured himself another drink.

The next morning, Julian woke up to the sound of somebody yelling his name in his ear. He groaned, wishing the noise would stop. His head was throbbing and he just needed to stay very still. He moved slightly, trying to investigate the noise. His earlier diagnosis had been incorrect, he was obviously dying. He clutched his head, a hand on either ear, trying to hold his head together.

The voice wouldn't shut up. "Jules, we have *Nutcracker* rehearsal, you have to get up now!"

Somebody's finger prised his eyelid open. "Jules?" the voice said softly. "You need to get up now, Mr. Yu won't wait for you."

Mao ... Keiko ... oh no! Mao said something to Keiko in Japanese and they both started giggling.

Julian wondered if he had enough strength to kick them out, and sat up with that aim in mind. He swore as his head registered the motion. His stomach lurched and he ran for the bathroom, Keiko and Mao following closely behind. He puked up all he could, then turned to the girls who were watching from the doorway with expressions of disgust. "Go away! It's rude to watch people hurl. Where's Leon?" He bent over the toilet again before they could answer.

"He went on the first trip with Mr. Yu to help with sets," Keiko said. "The show's today; how will you dance?"

Julian started to answer but interrupted himself: he had to bend over the toilet bowl again. That seemed to be it, so he locked the door so the girls couldn't come back. By the time he got out of the bathroom, the girls were all sitting in the kitchen ready to go. Keiko and Mao's buns were already perfectly done and Keiko was finishing up her nails.

"Hurry up," Mao said. "Mr. Yu's going to be here soon."

Julian gathered his stuff quickly. He reluctantly left his room when he heard everyone else calling him, sure that he had forgotten half of his stuff. They all piled into the van, the smell of old costumes, sets, and years of transporting Duan's buns gave it a peculiar smell that definitely would have made Julian puke if he hadn't seen the look on Mr. Yu's face. Julian steadied himself and lodged himself into the seat, clutching the side of the van in an attempt to anchor himself as the van started to move. The drive from Mr. Yu's house to The Centre had never felt so long.

Keiko patted him on the shoulder. "Yes, good boy don't ..." she paused, unsure.

"Puke?" Julian croaked.

Eventually, they reached The Centre, and Julian managed to clamber out, his legs had turned to jelly. They all walked into the theatre, Keiko pointing him in the direction of the boys' changing room. Nobody was there. Julian was grateful to be early. At that moment, Michael came bursting in.

"Oh, good, you're here! Tristan was looking for you. He thought that Mr. Yu was going to be late and you wouldn't have any time to warm-up before warm-up class. Are you okay? You look sick."

"I'm fine," Julian said very quietly, hoping that Michael would take the hint. "Where is everyone?"

"In the theatre, stretching. Right, you've never been here before have you? Come on, put on your warm-ups and I'll show you the way. You can help cut up the tinsel for the snow if you want. They always get the strands instead of the little pieces and have us cut them up because it's cheaper. It's fun, though."

Michael led Julian to the theatre and left him there, then ran off to see how Chloe and the rest were doing with the tinsel.

"Dude, come on." Tristan spotted Julian and called him over to where he was stretching his left splits on one of the audience's seats. "I can't believe that it's finally the show today. I'm so excited. I love how *The Nutcracker* just makes you feel like Christmas is finally here. Jules, are you okay?" Julian was lying, stomach down, on the carpet.

"I'm fine," Julian said, his voice muffled through the carpet. "Just a bit hung over."

"Hung over! Jules, it's the show today! What were you doing drinking? What are you going to do?"

Julian took a moment to sort out his thoughts. "I know, went with Mr. Yu, Dmitri, Jonathon, Leon, and some weird dude to Number Five. I dunno," he answered, without raising his voice above a whisper.

Tristan stared at him horrified. "Can you take something? Like … Aspirin? Would that work?" Julian just groaned.

Tristan got him some Aspirin and shoved both the pills and his water bottle into Julian's hand. "Take it!"

After they finished warming up, Alexandra turned to Tristan and said, "What's wrong with your BFF?" Julian had made it (sort of) through class, but he was now sprawled all over the floor again, blocking one of the aisles.

"Mr. Yu took him out drinking last night."

Taylor had gone over to Julian, and she bent down to talk to him. "Hey … you okay?"

"He's hung over," Tristan explained impatiently. Julian groaned.

"I think he's going to throw up or something," Tristan said, biting his lip worriedly.

"Oh, that sucks," Taylor said calmly. "Come on, Jules. Let's move you to the changing room, there's a bath-room there."

Tristan was annoyed. "You can't go in the boy's changing room. I'll take him."

"Since when?" Taylor asked, laughing. "Besides, I don't have rehearsal. I'll just take him." Jules got up. He was queasy as he followed her out of the theatre.

"Since when are they friends?" Tristan asked as he and Alexandra stared after them.

Alexandra shrugged. "Stretch my feet, Tris? Sweetie? My ankle's crap again today, and the cold outside is seriously not helping." Tristan bent over and began to stretch her feet in silence. "Thanks, love you forever," Alexandra said, concentrating on keeping her leg straight to take her mind off the pain.

Kageki came over and sat down next to them to stretch. "I'm so happy the show's today! And guess what? My parents can't fly over from Japan to watch me! It's so cool, yeah?"

Alexandra raised her eyebrows. "Kageki's parents are a bit scary," Tristan explained.

"Oh, sweet," Alexandra said. "Congratulations, then!"

Julian and Taylor came back in. Julian looked a bit better and he was drinking something.

Tristan quickly turned to Alexandra. "That bodysuit looks *so* hot on you, darling."

"Awe, you're so sweet! Love of my life...."

"I know, right?" Tristan bent over and kissed her on the mouth, and in a couple seconds they were doing a well-choreographed sex scene, rolling on the floor.

"Ugh, gross!" Kageki said, moving away from them. He hated it when Alexandra and Tristan got all weird.

"What are they doing down there?" Julian asked Taylor curiously. "I thought Tristan was gay."

"He is," Taylor confirmed. Keiko came toward them, so Taylor got up and gave Keiko her seat and then sat in Keiko's lap.

"Where's Dmitri?" Julian asked.

"Outside, having a smoke with Mr. Yu," said Keiko. "They won't be back for a couple of minutes probably; Mr. Yu was telling him a story. Taylor, your butt hurts!"

"Sorry," Taylor giggled. "I can't help it that I have a bony butt. I practically don't have a butt at all; I'm like so skinny!" Keiko didn't bother answering, just exchanged a meaningful look with Julian.

Kaitlyn was stretching by the door when Cecilia came into the theatre. "Mom, you're not supposed to be here!" she said, annoyed.

"I just wanted to talk to you. Just for a second. Come over here." Kaitlyn got up sulkily and went over to her. "Now, Kaitlyn, I want to film you in rehearsal so we can see if there is anything you need to work on. I already got permission from Gabriel, so don't give me any snits about it. Just go, do your best, and I'll film it for you."

"Gabriel can give permission for stuff? Since when? You are going to totally embarrass me. Thanks, Mom."

"Listen," Cecilia hissed. "You are very lucky you have me to do this for you, you know. Most mothers wouldn't do this. Most mothers wouldn't care. Do you know what most mothers do? They just stick the kid in school and ignore them. That's easy. I'd love to do that. Now you get that expression off your face and go work." Kaitlyn glared at her, cheeks burning, and went and sat down to stretch. Two of the younger girls were sitting there, too, and they stared at her as she sat down.

"I ... she was just telling me that she left my lunch in the changing room," Kaitlyn lied.

"Oh, Delilah!" Ella called to Delilah who was just coming into the theatre. She waved her over. "Come here. Sophia and I have to tell you something."

Delilah made her way over reluctantly, and was soon giggling with Ella and Sophia. "That's not too old!" she squealed loudly, causing everyone to turn in their direction.

Grace sighed and shook her head as she watched Delilah laugh with Ella and Sophia. "How does somebody that big manage to be that tiny?" she asked Anna. "I mean, look at her. "

"Proportion Distortion," said Anna. They both giggled.

"Oh, Aiko," Grace said, watching her walk past them to sit with Mao and a bunch of other Japanese students. "Will you sit with us? Pretty please?"

Aiko giggled. "Oh, of course, Grace-*Chan*." She went over by them and began to talk to them while doing *barre* work. After a couple of moments, the other Japanese girls came up and joined them, making them the largest and loudest group in the theatre since the little kids hadn't arrived yet. Grace smiled smugly, making sure that Alexandra noticed. Apparently she had: she had just climbed into Tristan's lap and was now artistically draped around him.

Just then Mr. Yu came striding in with Mrs. Castillo. He leaped onto the stage without hands. Mrs. Castillo tried to follow, but her advanced years and high heels meant that she nearly fell instead. Fortunately Mr. Yu grabbed her just before she fell and dragged her up on stage. They had a good chuckle up there and then Mr.

Yu cleared his throat. Everyone stayed perfectly silent, waiting for him to speak.

"Where is Mr. Moretti?" Mr. Yu asked, shading his eyes from the theatre lights as if he expected him to suddenly materialize in front of him.

"With Mr. Demidovski," Kageki called. Mr. Yu frowned unhappily. He got himself together and walked to the centre edge of the stage.

"Today we have photo-shoot. Put on your first-cast costumes. Then rehearsal, no costumes, but *pointe* shoes yes, mark stage. The younger students arrive soon. Then short break, forty-five minutes, maybe, to put on makeup, lunch, then show. Then dinner break, we will feed you Duan's buns, no need to leave theatre, and evening show. Okay? Understand?

"Today, you do nothing I not say you do. I say dance, you dance. I say go pee, you pee. No go to the bathroom when I say dance. You understand?" He tried not to smile.

"Yes," they chorused.

Alexandra rolled her eyes. "You hear that?" she asked Tristan, imitating Mr. Yu. "No go pee. Good dancer don't go pee."

"Oh?" Tristan said, imitating back. "Mrs. Castillo say pee, pee much then very skinny, great dancer."

"Ahh, but no pee on stage. Dancer must not pee on the stage, must only love on the stage," Alexandra said, laughing as she mixed up Mr. Demidovski and Mr. Yu.

"Go quick, get ready," Mr. Yu shouted, sending them all off to get changed.

Kaitlyn looked at herself in the changing room mirror. Her curls were perfect now. She wished that they didn't have to have the photo shoot and the evening show so far apart, they wouldn't stay perfect for that long.

Alexandra inclined her head in Kaitlyn's direction, looking at Grace and Anna, then shifted her focus to Chloe. Anna smiled and nodded. All three, plus Taylor, who wanted to see what was going on, went into the hallway.

"Chloe," Grace called sweetly. "Could you come here for a second?"

Chloe got up obediently and followed them down the hall. "What?"

"Oh, we just wanted to help you get ready in your Clara outfit," Alexandra explained, guiding her firmly down the hall to the green room where Cromwell Gilly was frantically making last minute alterations.

"But ... I'm not first cast."

"Oh, I don't think it really matters," Grace said. Anna snorted.

"And you look so much better in it than Kaitlyn does," Taylor added. The rest nodded, agreeing with her for once. They got her into the dress, and then they all headed to the stage to wait for the rest.

Kaitlyn hurried down the hall to the green room; if she didn't hurry she was totally going to be late. She looked through the racks and piles. Her costume wasn't there!

"Cromwell," she said, her voice tinged with panic, "Where is my costume?"

"What costume?"

"Clara!"

"Chloe's wearing it."

"But she's not first cast!" Kaitlyn was close to hysterics. Cromwell Gilly shrugged.

Kaitlyn flew to the stage. "You're late," Mr. Yu said disapprovingly.

"Chloe's wearing my costume! I'm first cast Clara, and she's wearing my costume!"

Mr. Yu sighed with impatience. "Chloe is wearing costume. You Clara, her Clara, doesn't matter. Go change into second cast costume or you will miss picture."

"I don't *have* a second cast costume. I'm not anything for second cast."

Mr. Yu shook his head impatiently. "Just go sit then. Have break."

Kaitlyn ran down the hallway and found a secluded stairway to bawl in. She pulled a mirror out of her bag. Awesome, her eyeliner was completely destroyed and her face was totally puffy. She wondered if it would be possible to stay sitting on those stairs until the show was over, to never see any of them again. She'd just sneak out the back door and disappear. She shook her head and snuck into the bathroom, fixing her face the best she could before rehearsal.

Rehearsal was the usual hectic mess. Mr. Yu had them do the second act first, and Mr. Moretti and Mr. Demidovski showed demanding to know why. Mr. Yu insisted that it made more sense for the sets that way. Mr. Moretti said that Mr. Yu was wasting his rehearsal time, and Mr. Yu said that he should have been there to start rehearsal himself if he was worried about wasting rehearsal time. Then he stalked off to fix the backdrops, calling Jonathon and Dmitri over to help. Mr. Moretti was infuriated because he had to call the boys over to rehearse every few seconds, and they wouldn't stay.

As they took their places for the Russian, Tristan noticed Kageki singing softly himself.

"Are you okay, Kageki?" Tristan asked.

"Yeah ... I just ... I didn't feel well? I am sick, and Jonathon gave me some American pills, and now I feel weird. But not sick!"

"What did you give Kageki?" Tristan asked Jonathon angrily. "Look at him." Kageki had a huge silly grin on his face and was wandering aimlessly around.

"What? He looks the same to me!" Jonathon said, but Tristan glared at him. "Okay, okay. I just gave him some painkillers. You know, it's kinda like Tylenol except stronger. I don't think they have it in Canada."

"Lovely! You've given him American drugs?" Tristan said angrily. "Thank God his parents aren't here. Dude, he's Japanese. Even I can't handle American pharmaceuticals, and I'm Canadian!"

After rehearsal, everyone went to get ready for the show.

"We need to start getting into makeup. Do you know even how to do it?" Tristan asked Julian as they started walking to the changing rooms, passing by Taylor and Keiko.

"Nope," said Julian. "Oh no! I forgot my makeup."

"It's okay, I'll loan you mine," Tristan reassured him.

At this Taylor popped up. "Tristan, it's okay, I'll loan him mine," she said brightly. "Because we have, like, the same skin colouring. I'll just get it. And I can help him put it on, because I don't have to get ready!" She ran off to get her makeup kit.

"I'll come, too," Keiko said. "Otherwise she'll put on too much."

"Thanks," Julian said gratefully. "I don't really need that much makeup. I mean, my eyelashes are totally long enough, I don't need mascara."

Tristan rolled his eyes. "Shut up, Julian!"

"What? They are."

Taylor came in waving her huge box of makeup. "I've got so much," she said happily.

"Caucasian eyes blink a lot," Keiko said as she attempted to put on Julian's eyeliner.

Alexandra sat in the girls' changing room, bored. She already had on all her makeup. She began adding a third layer just to fight her boredom and nervousness. All around her, everyone was talking excitedly, but she couldn't feel happy about the show. Her mind turned to the lunch in her bag, and she pulled out a Lara bar.

"You're hungry already?" Grace asked. "You're so calm! I couldn't eat a bite." She laughed a tinkling laugh.

Alexandra didn't bother to answer. She took her bag and found a quiet spot in one of the many halls. She ate quietly and quickly, afraid of being found before she was finished. When she finished, she stuffed the wrappers in her bag. *Oh, great,* she thought, fighting the tears that came to her eyes. She really hadn't wanted to do this today, it totally messed up her face and she really didn't have time. Well, it was too late, now. There was no way she could go out there and perform with all that in her stomach.

She pulled her shoes and jacket out of her bag and slipped them on. She left the theatre anxiously and crossed the street to the Starbucks, embarrassed since she had her bun in, wore several pounds of makeup and her multi-coloured warm-up pants. *What the hell, it's not as if it's going to stay in there.* She ordered a blueberry square and ate it quickly, fidgeting in her seat, worried that someone would come in and see her. Finally, she took out her water bottle and chugged the whole thing. She went to the bathroom and threw everything up. She took a toothbrush out of her bag and quickly brushed her teeth, trying to ignore the sounds of the lineup for the bathroom that appeared after she'd gone in.

Alexandra stepped outside of the Starbucks and into the fresh air, smiling as the cold wind touched her face. She ran across the street and slipped into the theatre again, feeling as if a load had been lifted off her mind.

There was total chaos when she stepped back into the changing rooms. There were little kids everywhere, and everyone was rushing around trying to organize their costumes. Alexandra noticed that one of the little kid's mothers had moved her makeup box and second bag off the counter and onto a chair. She angrily took the girl's stuff and moved it to the other side of the changing room, stuffing it beneath the counter. She stripped, having already put on her tights and second skin, and began to put on her first act costume.

"Excuse me," one of the mothers said. "Where have you put my daughter's stuff? Her stuff was right here, you can't move it!" Alexandra shrugged. "You moved it!"

"Excuse me? My stuff has been here since nine this morning. I have no idea what you're talking about. I have to get ready, you should probably go look for your daughter's stuff," she said, looking down at the little girl. *Definitely not going to be any good,* she thought. She turned around and began to put her snow headpiece on. "Why are all these little kid mothers in here?" she asked Mao loudly.

Mao shrugged. "I have no idea. They are not supposed to be here."

Mr. Yu came striding in. "First act, backstage in ten minutes," he announced, ignoring the fact that it was a girls' changing room. He looked at Alexandra's feet as she adjusted the ribbons on her *pointe* shoes. "No shiny," he said, tapping the box of her shoe.

"What!" they all wailed as he left.

"It's almost time and *now* he tells us 'no shiny'?" Alexandra said, angrily taking out her bottle of calamine lotion.

Aiko took out a container of powder. "It's okay, we can use this." She started to powder her shoes. Alexandra took her chances on the wet calamine. The powder looked slippery.

Kaitlyn walked out of the theatre and into the lobby, scanning the crowds of school kids for her mother. There she was at the door of the theatre, gesturing frantically. She quickly ran over. "So? How was it?"

"Shush, not right now," Cecilia whispered. "I'll tell you later." Kaitlyn sighed impatiently as they went to sit down.

"Oh, hi, Cecelia," Charlize said as she sat down. "Oh, and Kaitlyn! I forgot you weren't in the matinee anymore! I'm such a ditz! Isn't this nice? We've got seats next to each other."

"Yes," Cecilia said, smiling. "I didn't know you were going to be here. Kaitlyn said that Taylor isn't in the show this year."

"Yeah. Taylor decided that it was too much to do the show this year, she has just been working so hard on her *pas de deux* with Jules."

"Well, isn't that nice? I didn't know that Taylor was doing a *pas de deux* with him.... Well, good for her! She must be very excited. She's never done a *pas de deux* before, has she? I remember when Kaitlyn had her first. She was six, I think? She was *so* excited!" Kaitlyn slumped into her seat, bored as she listened to them battle it out. *I had better get a* pas de deux *with Jonathon*, she thought, inspecting the blister on her foot.

Julian looked in the mirror. His face seemed to have been transformed. "Wow. I look like an alien."

"No, you don't," Keiko said, insulted.

"It looks really good," Michael assured him as he carefully pencilled his eyebrows. "Very professional."

"I think you look totally hot!" Taylor said, giggling as she got out her camera and shoved it at Keiko. "Come on, picture time." She hopped down from the counter and wrapped her arms around Julian.

"*Ichi, ni, san* ..." Keiko said, carefully focusing the camera. "Oh, Tristan, you ruined it!" Tristan had stuck his hand, in a peace sign, in front of the camera right before she took the photo. The tried again. "Cute! You need to make this your profile pic," Keiko told Taylor, who quickly came to look.

"Aww, we take really good pictures together!" Taylor said, turning to Julian and smiling.

"My turn now." Tristan shoved his camera at Keiko. He wrapped his arms around Julian and smiled. Julian stuck his tongue out and winked at the camera.

"Cute," Keiko proclaimed.

Just then they heard the ten minute call.

"Oh no! I'm not finished!" Keiko squealed. She ran back to the girl's changing room.

The matinee went pretty well. Julian even got through the Russian without puking, and Kageki didn't sing except during the group bow. The kids were a fairly enthusiastic audience, enjoying everything except Dmitri and Grace's Sugarplum *pas de deux*, which received markedly lukewarm applause. The Russian was very popular, as was the snow, surprisingly enough.

The stage hands hadn't realized that the tinsel was supposed to be snow for two performances, or that it should be sprinkled gradually as opposed to being dumped in one huge tinsel flurry. Poor Aiko stepped out for a *pirouette diagonale* just as they dumped it, and fell. She got up quickly, but they were all slipping over the tinsel the rest of the dance, and Aiko had a huge clump of it in her hair. The snow corps came off stage frantically trying to shimmy the tinsel out of their tutus. After the bows there was a struggle to get off stage. The older students were trying to push their way through the dawdling little kids to the changing rooms, and Mr. Yu was frantically trying to sweep up the tinsel for the next performance. He was demanding that they all "Shake off! Shake off!" the tinsel that was all over them.

"Are the Duan's buns here yet?" Tristan asked Mr. Yu quietly as he passed him in the flood of bodies. Mr. Yu nodded. Tristan quickly mimed to the rest that the buns were there, and Kageki and Anna forced their way over to him. They made their way to the green room where the Duan's buns were set up on tables, picking up Taylor, Leon, and Jonathon on their way.

"Quickly," Tristan directed. "Taylor, you get the juice boxes, we'll get the buns." Taylor obediently got a couple flats of the juice. "To the boys changing room!" Tristan said quietly, his voice sharp with urgency. They made it to the boy's changing rooms without incident, and were greeted with a cheer.

"You made it!" Delilah crowed.

"Get what you want quick. They'll notice soon." They all began stacking buns on paper towel from the washroom and eating them.

"What's in them?" Julian asked.

"This is pork," Tristan said. "And this one is custard, and…"

"This one is egg and ham and stuff, and this one is coconut, its super sweet … like literally, in taste," Taylor interrupted. "And these are custard tarts, and these ones are raisin twisty bun things."

"Don't they want us to eat healthily?" Julian asked, taking a coconut bun. "They're always going on about being skinny. Where's the fruit platters?"

Tristan shrugged, taking the other half of Alexandra's bun as she reached in the box and took another.

"Do you think she knows that the calories still count, even if she splits with him?" Grace whispered to Anna.

Mr. Yu banged open the door and glared at them. They quickly shovelled almost all of the remaining buns onto the counter.

"Hi Mr. Yu," said Tristan.

"The parents," Mr. Yu said slowly, emphasizing the word parents with an expression of distaste, "say that you took all the buns." ·

A large man was practically jumping as he stood behind Mr. Yu, who was blocking him from entering the changing room. "Like they do every year!" he said, his voice high-pitched with excitement. "The older ones, they take the buns every year!"

"The parents aren't supposed to eat the buns," Tristan said defensively. "They always eat them."

Mr. Yu turned around to face the parents gathered in the hall. "The parents not supposed to eat the buns," he said sternly. "We pay for these buns, for the students." He tapped his chest to emphasize the seriousness of what he was saying. "They cannot go get dinner, they need to eat the buns. You, you don't have rehearsal, you can go spend the money, buy your own food."

"But the young children," one of the moms said. "They need to eat buns, too!"

Mr. Yu gave up. "Take them back out," he ordered. Tristan, Kageki, and Leon took the boxes back to the green room, now almost completely empty. Before they headed back they grabbed a small box of custard tarts, to protest by the parents.

Everyone slowly filed to their seats for the evening performance. The parents carefully smiled at some of the other parents, and pretended they didn't see others. Steven Audley came rushing in. Charlize grabbed him by the arm and led him to their seats. "Where were you?" she hissed. "I can't believe you were almost late."

"I was in a meeting!" He hissed back. "And Taylor isn't even dancing in this show."

Alison walked behind them, rolling her eyes. "Oh, look," she said excitedly "That's Julian's dad!" She pointed at a man with dreadlocks who looked like he was in his late twenties. He was wearing artistically distressed jeans and a black shirt with obviously hand painted words that said *"Find your own light"* underneath. Holding his hand was a beautiful naturally blond woman who looked like she was still in her teens. She wore no makeup, a tie-dyed tank top, knee-high boots, and a loose, swirly purple skirt that stopped half an inch before her boots. Holding on to her other hand was a small blond boy who looked about five, with huge dimples. He started waving to everyone, happy about all the attention he was generating.

"What?" Charlize said. "That can't be Julian's dad, he's way too young. And how do you even know what Julian's dad looks like?"

"Taylor showed me his Facebook page."

"Is that his mother then?" Charlize asked in disbelief, watching as the trio made their way to their seats.

"No, that's Julian's dad's girlfriend," Alison said. "And that must be his half brother, River."

"Well, we'll have to say hello, then."

"Not me," Steven said, snorting. He went to sit down.

Charlize and Alison went over to the trio, and Charlize offered her hand to Julian's dad, saying "Hi, I'm Charlize, Taylor's mom. You must be Julian's family?"

Julian's dad smiled and shook her hand. "Yup. I'm Will, and this is my partner Daisy and our son River."

"I'm Viver!" River confirmed, smiling.

"Well, it's so nice to meet you!" Charlize said as Taylor came into the theatre, running towards them in her high heels and tiny black dress.

"Oh, are you Julian's parents?" she asked, giggling.

"Yes, honey, this is Julian's dad," Charlize said, placing a hand on her shoulder.

"Hi, Mr. Reese," Taylor said, waving excitedly even though they were a maximum of three feet from each other.

"Oh please, call me Will," he said, uncomfortably staring at Taylor's chest. "Nobody ever calls me Mr. Reese."

Taylor had made friends with River as her mom talked to Will and Daisy. "I'm going to go backstage to watch. Can I take River with me, Daisy?"

"Taylor, I hardly think that …" Charlize began to protest but Daisy cut her off.

"Sure! River would like that. Have fun, River," Daisy said, her voice sounding unusually mellow.

River jumped off his seat and Taylor took his hand. They both went off without a backwards glance, River explaining to Taylor as they went that "I am very good at soccer. And painting."

Jeff and Cecilia Wardle sat in the centre middle seats, surrounded by relatives, friends they'd roped into coming, and Mrs. Mallard. Mrs. Mallard was explaining loudly that "Kaitlyn just has so much better technique than the rest of the academy. I try, I do my best, but good clean technique just isn't *valued* at the academy. I've talked to the Demidovskis about it many times, and every time, Mrs. Demidovski says that she will talk to the teachers. But nothing ever changes! And you know what? It's the students who suffer, it's the students." Cecilia smiled sympathetically and led the conversation back to the subject of Kaitlyn's Solo Seal examination.

Peter and Beth Dunstan were sitting with Tristan's parents. "Tristan is really inspired to go to the Genee competition after Alexandra found it so enriching," Kaveri Patel was saying.

"That's good," Beth said, scanning the room for Grace and Anna's parents. "I'm sure he will find it a marvellous opportunity." There they were! She pressed her lips together, seeing that the Kendalls and the Valaraos were talking excitedly.

The evening show was better simply because of Aiko's wonderful job on the Sugarplum *pas de deux* and variation. The snow was dropped correctly this time, thanks to Mr. Yu's screaming into the crews' headsets. Michael made a very touching Fritz. But Kaitlyn was wearing soft shoes, for some reason.

Cecilia ran backstage during intermission. "What happened? Why are you in soft shoes?"

Mr. and Mrs. Demidovski were right behind her. "Must be on *pointe*! Must be proper shoes!" Mrs. Demidovski thundered.

Kaitlyn struggled not to cry, her eyes welling up. "Somebody poured water all over my *pointe* shoes!"

"What! You only bring one pair?" Mrs. Demidovski demanded, not at all shocked by this revelation. "Where is Chloe?"

Cecilia whipped out a pair of shoes from her purse. "Here you are, Kaitlyn. I just finished sewing them."

"But they're brand new!" Kaitlyn protested, her eyes welling again.

Cecilia glared at her. "She can wear these," she said, smiling at Mr. and Mrs. Demidovski. Mr. Demidovski nodded in agreement, and they both left.

In the second act, Alexandra managed to look beautiful in the Arabian despite a slightly fixed smile. Julian, quite frankly, looked like he was going to puke during dolls: Mao was practically holding him up instead of the other way around. He did one less jump than he was supposed to in Russian, but he ended up looking good in spite of himself. Tristan shone, looking completely professional and lighting up the stage with his smile. He managed to look very much in love with Kaitlyn, as well, which was a bit hard to do as she was dancing with zero expression and was extremely unsteady during their *pas de deux* thanks to her un-broken-in shoes. Dmitri looked like he was marking the whole show, and at the end while everyone was standing on stage and the audience was clapping, he mouthed, "Do you want to go for a drink?" to Jonathon, apparently unaware that the audience could still see him. Kageki nearly made it through the show without mishap, but he collapsed into giggles as they took their bows.

Certain members of the audience had been drinking heavily during intermission, as Mr. Demidovski had predicted, and as the audience waited for him to make his speech they discussed the show.

"Grace's thighs are quite a bit bigger than that Arabian girl's, don't you think, Paula?" Grace's grandfather commented. "I quite enjoyed that Arabian dance. Very sexy and all that." April Kendall glared at him.

"Which one was Kaitlyn, again?" Steven Audley asked loudly.

Charlize Petrenko shushed him, looking around to make sure that Cecilia Wardle hadn't heard.

Finally, Mr. Demidovski made his way up to the stage. He cleared his throat. "Everyone … clap for the students! They have given us a beautiful show!" He turned around to the students. "Everyone … clap for your parents! They make all of this possible." He launched into a lecture on the importance of parents starting their child's dance education early, the importance of the arts, the value of supporting a child who wanted to be a dancer, and the need for donations to the school. Then he thanked all of the teachers individually. The dancers stood on stage, clapping when told to, zoning out otherwise. The littlest ones began yawning. Finally, he began thanking some of the students individually. "Alexandra! She won the bronze in the international competition this year!" Gabriel whispered in his ear. "The Genee International Competition."

River had been perfectly happy sitting on Taylor's lap backstage during the show, finding the whole thing fascinating, but now he was getting bored. "Can I go see Jules? I will be just there." He pointed onstage where Julian was standing next to Tristan, swaying sleepily.

"Just a bit longer," Taylor whispered, tugging him back onto her lap. She pulled a packet out of her purse. "Look, here's some chocolate."

"Is it dairy?" River asked, looking up at her.

"Uh ... no," said Taylor, not sure what exactly was classified as dairy. River smiled, quite willing to be bribed, and began to eat it.

Mr. Demidovski had reached Kaitlyn. "And, our Clara!" he proclaimed grandly. "Karen is new at the academy, but she does very well. Yes, very well!" The older students woke up at this and began sniggering. Mr. Demidovski was finally finished, and they all clapped for the last time as the curtains started to close. They waited until the curtains had completely closed, and then started screaming and jumping around, hugging each other, all the adrenaline of the night coming out in an exuberant rush. Taylor grabbed River's hand and tried to keep up with him as he began to run to Julian, yelling "Jules! I'm here!"

"River!" Julian shouted excitedly. He swooped him up in his arms. "Where are Will and Daisy?"

"I don't know," River said, shrugging his shoulders. "I'm with Tay. Tay's my girlfriend."

Taylor blushed. "No, I'm your friend that's a girl."

"Thanks for bringing him," Julian said, smiling at her as they were shoved to the changing rooms in the press of people. Julian introduced River to everyone, and River was clearly in his element, enjoying the height he achieved in Julian's arms. They passed Mr. and Mrs. Demidovski.

"Ah, your brother?" Mr. Demidovski asked, inclining his head toward River.

"Yep, this is River."

"And how did you like the show, River?"

"It was good!"

Mr. Demidovski laughed and shook River's hand. "Thank you," he said seriously.

They continued on their way to the changing rooms, Taylor bobbing happily along in the wake left behind Julian and River. Everyone was congregated in the boy's changing rooms to take pictures and say their goodbyes before Christmas holidays. The little kids and their parents had taken over the girl's changing room.

"Guys, guys, listen!" Jessica suddenly shouted in a panic. "We forgot Secret Santa!" Everyone quickly ran, got their presents out of their bags, and began to hand them out.

Kaitlyn waited expectantly. Secret Santa was always so exciting. She'd gotten Chloe, and handed her a pair of warm-up booties. "Oh, thanks Kaitlyn, you're sweet," Chloe gushed. "Come on; take a picture with me and the booties!"

After all the Secret Santa gifts had been handed out, everyone started to pack up. Taylor was sitting on the counter with River, taking pictures. They both found this highly entertaining, and Taylor was very impressed that River already knew how to flash a peace sign at the camera.

"Again," he'd command every time she stopped taking pictures.

"No, let's film now," said Taylor, showing him how it worked.

Kaitlyn looked around impatiently. She hadn't gotten a Secret Santa gift. "Jessica," she said, walking over to her. "Who's my Secret Santa? Did I not have one?"

"Everyone had a Secret Santa," Jessica said, staring at her like she was out of her mind. "Maybe yours just forgot."

"Forgot? How could you forget about Secret Santa? Don't you have a list or something so I could check who it was? "

"No," Jessica said curtly. "I have no idea who it was. It's not such a big deal, it's only Secret Santa. Don't be such a baby." She turned her back to Kaitlyn and began buttoning up her coat. As she walked out the door, Kaitlyn stared after her in disbelief. She picked up her bag and left to go find her parents, fighting not to cry.

Julian finally came out of the washroom. "I can't get the makeup off." His voice was tinged with fear. "This eyeliner is, like, permanent."

Tristan rolled his eyes. "Dude, it's called makeup remover for a reason!" He handed him the bottle and some swabs.

"Thanks, man," Julian said with relief.

"'Night guys," Alexandra said, smiling brightly. "See you after the holidays." She gave Julian and Tristan hugs, waved at River, and ignored Taylor. "Have fun moving sets," she added, smirking at Tristan before she walked out the door, her mouth trembling with the effort to keep up her smile.

"Thanks," Tristan called after her sarcastically. Everyone else slowly trickled out.

"Don't you have to go home, Taylor?" Julian asked. "I can take River."

"It's okay. I think he's gone to sleep." She stared down at River, proudly. He was flopped in her arms, chocolate smeared all over his face and some melting in his pocket, still clutching Taylor's camera and snoring loudly. At that moment he gave a snuffle and leaned closer to Taylor, getting chocolate on her dress.

"Julian, aren't your parents here?" Tristan asked.

"Yeah," Julian said, putting on his shoes.

"So ... aren't you staying with them tonight? I can just tell Mr. Yu that you can't help move sets because your parents said you have to go."

"Good one! Thanks Tristan, see you after the holidays, bro." He gave him a hug.

"Sure, see you Jules, have fun," Tristan said awkwardly. He picked up his bags and went to help Mr. Yu. As he walked through the door, he tripped on a stray wire. He got up, blushing. "Bye!"

"Bye bye, Tristan," Taylor said happily as he finally left.

"Want me to take him?" Julian asked, holding his hands out for River.

Taylor let Julian take him and then hopped off the counter, shaking her arms. "He gets heavier when he goes to sleep."

Julian laughed. "Little lump," he said, looking down at his brother fondly. They walked into the hall.

"*Juulliaan,*" Cromwell Gilly said from down the hall. He had an uncharacteristically dreamy expression on his face. "My dear boy, how did you manage to escape the immovable Mr. Yu?" He was sitting on one of the costume trunks, with Anna and Alexandra's older brothers. "We really must move these," Cromwell giggled, looking up at them.

Justin just smiled at him. Taylor wrinkled her nose. "I think I'm high just smelling the air around them! Poor River."

"Don't worry," Julian said, chuckling as he looked down at River. "He's used to it."

They walked through the theatre doors and spotted their parents, standing at opposite ends of the cluster of people. "Well … bye," Julian said awkwardly.

"Bye," said Taylor brightly. She gave him a big hug. "Have a good Christmas break." She stood on her *demi-pointe* and kissed River on the cheek. "Bye, Viver," she said softly, and then ran to join her parents.

TAKE A SNEAK PEEK AT THE NEXT BALLET SCHOOL CONFIDENTIAL BOOK, *YOU'RE SO SWEET*

Julian Reese
does NOT have Bieber hair. And is going back to Van today — hopefully.

"Will?"

Will didn't look up. His headphones were plugged into his laptop, and he was bopping in time to the music as he worked on his blog. It was a marvellous work concerning the philosophy of the world, as translated by William O. Reese. Julian sighed and waved his hand in front of his father's face.

"What?" Will turned to Julian.

"You said you would drive me to the ferry, remember?"

"Yes, but— Hey, dude, do you think you could ask Daisy if she'd take you? It's just … I'm really in the zone here."

"Daisy's working at the farmer's market," Julian explained. "It's Sunday, remember?"

"Oh, yeah …"

River came in and wrapped his arms around Julian's legs. "Are you leaving, Jules?"

"Yeah." Julian looked down at his little brother. "I have to go back to dance, remember?"

"Why can't you dance here?"

"Because I can't, little guy. Now shush for a sec, all right? Will, I really need to go now. Like, *now*."

"Oh. Okay, let's go, you guys tell me when you're ready, and we'll go, okay?"

"We're ready," Julian assured him.

River stuck out his foot. "My shoes are already on, even."

Making his way onto the ferry bound for Vancouver, Julian was still running things he wished he could say to his dad through his mind. He hurried through the ferry lounges, trying to find a seat.

And of course the ferry is completely packed. Great ... Julian headed for a relatively clear place on the ferry floor and sat down. His iPod wasn't loud enough to drown out the noises of the cranky passengers around him. *Will's probably still furious with me for losing his blog post when I unplugged the computer.* Julian flipped restlessly through the songs on his iPod. A year ago he wouldn't have minded his dad's carefree attitude towards time, River, or himself, but a year was a long time. His phone vibrated with a text from Taylor.

"Hey, u catch the 5?"
"No Im on the 7"
"K. See u at 830ish"

That was another problem — Taylor. He was grateful that she was going to pick him up and everything, but ... *Maybe I'm just being a jerk. So what if Taylor is annoying? At least she tries to be a good friend.* That was the problem with Taylor really: she tried too hard. Julian swung himself up from the ferry floor. The line up for the cafeteria was disgustingly long, but he was starving.

Fries in hand, he wandered up to the top deck, thinking. He was sure that Will had been better when he was young, but the way Will was with River ... *well, carefree wasn't the right word. Lazy? Maybe it's because River looks more like Daisy than Will.* And it was not like Daisy was any sort of mom at all, the only thing Julian had seen her do for River all Christmas break was when they'd gone to her parents' house for Christmas dinner and she'd taken all the turkey off his plate. Julian shook his head, remembering. *It's all right to raise the kid vegan, but most of the time Daisy forgets to feed him, period.* Julian scowled out at the ocean, watching as the rain beat down on the black waves and ferry deck. It was already dark, and the weather seemed to be getting worse. Freezing, he went back inside and sat down on the floor again, the rain from his coat dripping on the ferry carpet.

Finally the ferry arrived at Horseshoe Bay. Julian half ran down the walkway, weaving expertly through the tired passengers. Hurriedly scooping his suitcase from the luggage carousel, he went outside, anxiously scanning the crowd for Taylor and Charlize.

"Jules, Jules, over here!" Taylor called, waving excitedly.

Relieved, Julian half-ran, half-walked over, breaking into a grin. "Hey Taylor!"

"I missed you! I'm so, so excited for classes again, aren't you? Did you have fun with your family? How is River? They must've missed you, hey? Mom is, like, so stupid, she forgot how to get to Horseshoe Bay, and so we were, like, almost late, and then you would've been waiting in the dark here for us. It's so friggin' freezing out. Mom, could you *please*, like, turn on the heat? We're completely freezing?"

Julian got into the car, sinking into the seat. "Hey, Allison," he said smiling at Taylor's little sister. Allison grinned at him, not bothering to unplug her earbuds.

"So Julian, Taylor said that you two were thinking of doing a *pas* together?" Charlize said as she made her way up the curving road onto the highway into Vancouver.

"Oh, yeah."

"I was thinking, we should probably do two," Taylor said. "That way we could do a contemporary *pas* and a classical."

"Uh, that sounds good," Julian agreed, but he was slightly unsure. "The only thing is, do these *pas de duexs*, do we have to pay for them?"

"Well, there's an entry fee … but, we can see how it goes. We can like, talk about it later, right? But it would be fun, right?"

"Yeah."

Taylor chattered aimlessly the rest of the way into Vancouver, and Julian smiled and nodded where necessary until they finally dropped him off at Mr. Yu's house.

Look for Book Two of the
BALLET SCHOOL CONFIDENTIAL
series at your favourite bookseller in 2012.